was born Elizabeth Coles in Reading, Berkshire, in 1912. The daughter of an insurance inspector, she was educated at the Abbey School, Reading, and after leaving school worked as a governess and, later, in a library. At the age of twenty-four she married John William Kendall Taylor, a businessman, with whom she had a son and a daughter.

Elizabeth Taylor wrote her first novel, *At Mrs Lippincote's* (1945), during the war while her husband was in the Royal Air Force. This was followed by *Palladian* (1946), *A View of the Harbour* (1947), *A Wreath of Roses* (1949), *A Game of Hide-and-Seek* (1951), *The Sleeping Beauty* (1953), *Angel* (1957), *In a Summer Season* (1961), *The Soul of Kindness* (1964), *The Wedding Group* (1968), *Mrs Palfrey at the Claremont* (1971) and *Blaming*, published posthumously in 1976. She has also published four volumes of short stories: *Hester Lilly and Other Stories* (1954), *The Blush and Other Stories* (1958), *A Dedicated Man and Other Stories* (1965) and *The Devastating Boys* (1972). Elizabeth Taylor has written a book for children, *Mossy Trotter* (1967); her short stories have been published in the *New Yorker, Harper's Bazaar, Harper's* magazine, *Vogue* and the *Saturday Evening Post*, and she is included in *Penguin Modern Stories 6*.

Elizabeth Taylor lived much of her married life in the village of Penn in Buckinghamshire. She died in 1975.

Critically Elizabeth Taylor is one of the most acclaimed British novelists of this century, and in 1984 *Angel* was selected as one of the Book Marketing Council's "Best Novels of Our Time". Virago publish eight of her sixteen works of fiction.

⌐PALLADIAN⌐

ELIZABETH TAYLOR

With a New Introduction by
Paul Bailey

PENGUIN BOOKS – VIRAGO PRESS

PENGUIN BOOKS
Viking Penguin Inc., 40 West 23rd Street,
New York, New York 10010, U.S.A.
Penguin Books Ltd, Harmondsworth,
Middlesex, England
Penguin Books Australia Ltd, Ringwood,
Victoria, Australia
Penguin Books Canada Limited, 2801 John Street,
Markham, Ontario, Canada L3R 1B4
Penguin Books (N.Z.) Ltd, 182–190 Wairau Road,
Auckland 10, New Zealand

First published in Great Britain by Peter Davies 1946
First published in the United States of America by
Alfred A. Knopf Inc. 1947
This edition first published in Great Britain by Virago Press Ltd 1985
Published in Penguin Books 1985

Copyright Elizabeth Taylor, 1946
Copyright renewed Elizabeth Taylor, 1974
Introduction copyright © Paul Bailey, 1985
All rights reserved

ISBN 0 14 016.113 9

Printed in Great Britain by
Cox & Wyman at Reading, Berkshire
Set in Baskerville

To
MY HUSBAND

INTRODUCTION

ELIZABETH TAYLOR's second novel, *Palladian*, was first published in 1946 and "produced in conformity with the authorised economy standards", as books were at that grim time. The title must have sounded particularly sumptuous in Sir Stafford Cripps's Britain, with its suggestion of the grand architecture of the eighteenth century. Yet "Palladian" has other meanings, it should be remembered—to do with learning and wisdom; the wisdom of ancient Greece, of the virgin Pallas Athena. The hardships in *Palladian* are those endured by the human heart, and are constant. They are not to do with the after-effects of war—the bombed houses, the bread queues, the food rationing.

Those nasty local difficulties can be found in a notable novel which came out in the same year—*Back* by Henry Green. It is one of the many oddities of the literary life that Green, who was apolitical but voted Tory because he feared the alternatives, should have written—albeit allusively—about the immediate issues of the day, while Elizabeth Taylor, who was an active Communist in the 1930s and a staunch Labour supporter for the rest of her life, chose to set *Palladian* in an England few people could recognize. Her hero is a man of leisure whose principal activity is to read the Greek classics in the original. He lives in a decaying country mansion (country mansions have been decaying in English fiction almost since they were built) with a large garden, complete with statuary. He is handsome, he is a widower, and his name is Marion. Who ever heard of a man called Marion? Howard Marion Crawford was a popular radio actor of the period, of course—but somehow that robust Howard made the more effete Marion acceptable. He had, I recall, a voice redolent of tweed suits and tobacco. But *Marion Vanbrugh* . . .

I doubt very much if there were many Cassandras around in the 1940s either. Cassandra Dashwood is our heroine here, a bookish girl with a need to fall in love, which she swiftly proceeds to do—with the man who employs her to act as governess to his child, Sophy. No prizes, as they say, for guessing his identity: step forward, Marion Vanbrugh. Elizabeth Taylor is quite shameless in the way she adheres to the formulae of romantic tosh, for Cassie is an orphan on the look-out for an older man, a substitute for the darling Daddy she misses so much, and it would be a cruel authoress indeed who didn't manoeuvre that fated meeting between the pretty virgin and the worldly-wise father-figure. It's with the character of the latter that Elizabeth Taylor, who wasn't an *authoress*, sneakily hints that she is playing ironic games within her novelettish plot. Marion *is* effete, his good looks are womanish, in the manner of the English upper classes, and worldly-wise he isn't. He is what Margaret Thatcher would deem a "wet", and livelier girls than Cassandra dismiss as a "drip". Almost the first thing he does after meeting his future bride is to offer her Greek lessons. Does she accept? Naturally. Later in the story, he gives her a glass of fine sherry, but does not replenish that glass when she shows signs of tipsiness. A cad would have done precisely that, and then carried the hapless orphan off to an upper room, where . . . But that is another kind of tosh altogether.

There are several clues planted throughout *Palladian* for the astute reader—clues which amount to evidence of Elizabeth Taylor's ultimate intentions in this strange little novel. Her favourite writer, Jane Austen, is invoked in a dozen different ways—"Cassandra Dashwood", for a start; the insinuating references to *Northanger Abbey* and *Mansfield Park*; the fact that the MGM film of *Pride and Prejudice* is showing at the cinema in the nearby town. As in an Austen novel, young Cassandra and middle-aged Marion will make the perfect pair. She is a sensible girl and he is a decorous lover who has been wounded by the loss of his wife. Their eventual union is a foregone conclusion, a simple fact which need not deter anyone from reading *Palladian*, for I am revealing nothing of importance. The surprises are all on the periphery of that central, familiar theme.

The servants get a look-in, for example, as they don't in Jane Austen, except by implication. Elizabeth Taylor has a wonderful time with the vengeful old Nanny:

She had taken her standards from lives of idleness and plenty and despised those who worked for their living, and could not pick up a duster now without a feeling of being lowered in her own eyes.

And, superbly:

Nanny feigned eccentricity as Hamlet feigned part of his madness, and for more or less the same reason, so that she could speak her mind, set herself apart from humanity and tell the truth, keep her integrity in words, at least, and have every allowance made.

This is the real world beyond Cassandra and Marion, who function on a more obviously *literary* plane. Nanny's snobbishness is beautifully caught, for being so exact, and her preference for male babies (the female ones are despised from birth onwards) rings horribly true, and also accounts for some of the peculiar sexual practices the English gentry still indulge in.

"Half the world scrubbing on their knees, the other half sitting on its arse": thus speaks Mrs Adams, the far-from-thorough cleaner who offends Nanny by having a baby daughter and by being of the lower orders, too. The two women have some spirited, if laconic, conversations:

"I like a nice Sunday film myself," said Nanny, "but as things are I couldn't go."

"Technicolour," said Mrs Adams, peeling potatoes at the sink.

"I can never settle down to technicolour. Some of those blue skies are cruel. An artist wouldn't paint pictures like that. If he did he'd be disqualified."

"It gives more idea of the dresses."

"That I'll grant you . . ."

Lovely stuff, the more amusing because it is kept in check and not allowed to run on purposelessly.

"Tom could not bear stoicism in those he hurt, could not bear the guilt of forcing them into such courage": that sentence is typical of the later Elizabeth Taylor of the incomparable short stories, of *Mrs Palfrey at the Claremont* and *The Wedding Group*. Tom is the most interesting person in *Palladian*, if only because the reason for his excessive drinking is not disclosed until very near the end of the book. His sudden lapses into acute boredom are very well done, as is the casual cruelty he displays towards the woman he reluctantly takes as his mistress—the publican's wife, Mrs Veal. Their slightly grubby liaison is a further reminder that Cassandra and Marion are among the charmed and blessed.

There is a marvellous short scene towards the close of *Palladian*, where Mrs Veal finally chats with Tom's sarcastic and distinctly uppity sister, Margaret. Mrs Veal, in her frustration, says something that brings in its wake the final loss of hope, without which no relationship, however squalid or one-sided, can continue to exist. It's a desolating moment, in a novel that is frequently artificial and self-conscious. What happens to Sophy is stagey by comparison. I shall not reveal what happens to Sophy, since it is designed to surprise, and does so.

Two worlds collide, then, in this flawed work: the world of cultivated leisure, where old books do also furnish a room; a world the young Elizabeth Taylor (young in terms of novel-writing, that is) could have some teasing fun with by deliberately fashioning it to suit her own purpose, and that other, larger world out there, in which hurt and humiliation take their daily toll. The result is a fairy-story of sorts, with a happy ending for only two of its participants.

"The walls were correctly hung with 'The Rake's Progress', in keeping with the gentility of the place", writes Elizabeth Taylor, describing the vestibule of a hotel. Just consider the way she uses that word "gentility", remember what "The Rake's Progress" really depicts, and you will understand the materials of which her art is composed. What a marvel of a sentence it is, and how many of its kind and quality she set down, this writer who had "gentility" slung at her again and again by those too blind to see her darker, subtler purpose.

Paul Bailey, London, 1984

CHAPTER ONE

CASSANDRA, with all her novel-reading, could be sure of experiencing the proper emotions, standing in her bedroom for the last time and looking from the bare windows to the unfaded oblong of wall-paper where 'The Meeting of Dante and Beatrice' in sepia had hung for thirteen years above the mantelpiece.

The room had quite changed, was curiously smaller without its furniture and, uncurtained, seemed defenceless against the stares of people on the tops of trams outside.

She flung up the sashed pane and leant her elbows on the stone sill. She had knelt there on many evenings, watching the pattern of people in the street, the cyclists free-wheeling down the dip in the road, the tram-lines running with gold in the sunset (for do we not think of the summers of our lives?), and with every nerve responding to and recording for her ever after the sound of the shop-doors opening and shutting across the road (the continual *ping* of one door bell after another), the paper-boy yelling in the gutter, the trams like absurd and angry monsters roaring under the railway bridge. She smelt the sooty garden below, the dusty privet, full of old mauve and white tram tickets, could see a line of trucks shunted across the bridge, and knelt there, listening to, snuffing up the life of the little piece of street, from bridge to the corner where the trams stopped. With her fingers she began from long habit to prise off the little feet of the virginia creeper, which sucked close to the stone sill like limpets upon rocks.

Kneeling on the bare boards by the window, she felt as if some hand, enormous, omnipotent, were wrenching her out

of her environment, prising her away, as she had the creeper
from its background, and pity for herself alternated with the
sudden knowledge that another evening in the same place
was not to have been borne.

One tram after another racketed by and left sometimes a
dribble of people, soon dispersed, at the street corner. From
one of these little crowds a woman separated herself and
came without hesitation towards the gate. Oddly foreshortened she appeared from the bedroom window. The bell-
ringing seemed to wind upwards through the empty house.
Cassandra pulled down the sash and ran downstairs. A
shape moved beyond the blue and ruby glass of the front
door.

"Ah, I've managed to catch you," said the woman. "Is
your mother in?"

"My mother is dead, I'm afraid."

"Well, dad, then. Whoever's in charge."

"My father died a fortnight ago." ('I'm sorry you missed
him,' she managed to prevent herself saying in an excess of
nervous courtesy.) "There is no one but me . . . I."

The woman swept aside her attempts to speak correctly
as her father would have wished. "I saw you moving out
this morning when I was across at the butcher's. Is the house
let, can you tell me? I didn't want to miss the chance for my
daughter. Perhaps you'd give me the name of the landlord?"

She handed pencil and old envelope at once, and Cassandra, resting the paper against the smoothish stone of the
porch, began to write.

"How many rooms downstairs, did you say?"

"I . . . well, there are three."

"And bedrooms?"

"Four bedrooms. And a cellar. A coal cellar. They
tip it down through that grating . . . the coal, I mean."

6

She pointed, but the woman looked down the passage instead.

"What sort of cooker?"

"A range."

The woman frowned, clicked her tongue. "That won't suit Ivy. Perhaps I could just give it a glance." She led the way down the passage. Cassandra followed helplessly.

"You leaving this lino?"

"Yes."

"Silly. It's no use to Ivy. She's got her own."

"The furniture's gone to be sold. It's no use to me either."

"Silly, though. Lino always goes well at an auction— even odd pieces. Next to chests of drawers, I can't think of anything that goes better."

While the woman stopped over the kitchen-range, rattling the dampers, examining flues, Cassandra looked out of the dirty window at the three little trees she had grown from chestnuts, set in diminishing heights and covered now with their bursting sticky buds. She had meant to plant one on each of her birthdays, but had soon forgotten.

"Ivy won't make much of this. Did you do all your cooking on it?" She looked at Cassandra with a new expression on her face, of wonderment, perhaps, or respect.

"Well, after my mother died, my father and I seemed to live on bread-and-butter."

The look faded.

If she had worn a diamond ring Cassandra could have cut her name on the window-pane, to impress something of her personality on the house. As it was, she wrote her initials in the dust, and brushed her fingers on her skirt.

"Well, I must be away," said the woman. "I'll just peep into the other rooms as I go out. Leave the upstairs for now."

Cassandra turned the back-door key and followed.

" Well, all these shelves? " The woman stood in the little room and stared.

" My father's books."

" Well, we'd have to pull all that down, of course. It needs re-papering. They take a good foot off the room all the way round. How many books did he have, then? "

" He had two thousand," Cassandra said, suddenly whitening with fatigue and leaning against the door.

The dirtyish room, with its dusty shelves and the fringe of ivy round the window, filled her with unhappiness—this room in which her father had lain in his coffin, the submarine light of the sun through a bottle-green blind, the green-filled room, the books dimmed and shadowy, the flowers round the coffin even pink and fleshy like water-flowers, and wreaths lying on chairs drowned-looking with their pale shell-colours.

The next room was all right; it had been merely the front-room where her mother had sat at her sewing machine, a noisy room from the street and the trams, and bright now, like another world, with the evening sunlight.

" Yes, well, I'll go round and see the landlord, since you say you've heard nothing."

" I'll come with you," said Cassandra suddenly, picking up a case from the hall and, without glancing round again, following the woman out and slamming the door. " I have to take the keys." ('I couldn't stay there alone one second longer,' she told herself.)

'That's that,' she also thought, going along beside the railings with the woman. ' Not even a good-bye—not a tear. Bang the door quickly after thirteen years and walk out with a stranger. And not a moment for any of the thoughts I meant to have.'

.   .   .   .   .

" I do feel a course of Sanatogen is the thing for you," said Mrs Turner. " You don't seem in a fit state to . . . let me just . . . one moment . . ." She put aside her coffee cup and leant forward and pulled down Cassandra's lower eyelid. " I remember when Helen was your age . . . Come in ! What is it, Alma? Oh, the post ! You can just run to the corner, but put on your cloak, dear. Oh, and Alma ! Ah, never mind, she's gone. It doesn't matter. Yes, Helen ! She must have been twenty. I know she was at Somerville at the time, because it was such a pity . . ."

Cassandra leant back in Mrs Turner's rocking-chair, dreaming, half-listening, as she had for years. ' Cups of tea . . . Sanatogen . . . Benger's . . . Change your damp stockings.' Even the spirit attended to, but with a domestic helpfulness. " I *do* think you'd feel ever so much more comfortable in yourself if you would come to church." Outside, in the school garden, girls went by in their long green cloaks, against the sad landscape of playing-field and leafless poplars.

" And your aunt has gone? " Mrs Turner was asking.

" Yes, this morning. I had some clearing up to do."

" But it was dismal for you there by yourself, dear. You should have come round to lunch ; or tea, at least. You could have managed that. I sometimes think you have a tendency towards sadness, Cassandra. You need more pleasure, and I rather wonder how you will contrive to get it at the Vanbrughs. You really do need taking out of yourself . . . and I don't remember Margaret Vanbrugh being so very gay . . . of course, she and Helen parted after they left school and Helen went to Somerville and Margaret to London . . . and then you know how it is . . . but I imagine she was sensible rather than gay when she was a girl. The cigarettes are just beside you . . . or would you like a bar of chocolate? "

Lulled into peace, Cassandra lay back in her chair. The gas fire roared unevenly in its broken white ribs. Mrs

Turner's wedding-group hung crookedly where and as it always had, and a curtain flapped idly over the papers on the writing-table, which were pretty well held down, however, by pieces of stone from the Acropolis.

"It must be time for prayers . . ." Mrs Turner rose and smoothed—or hoped to smooth—her skirt, and, standing before the mirror, twisted one frond of hair after another into the supporting combs and stabbed-in hairpins and patted gently. "Are you coming in, dear? I think it would be rather nice before you go away . . . unless you are tired and would . . . I expect you are very tired . . . stay quietly here and when I come back Ethel shall bring us some Benger's . . . ah, there's the bell."

"But I should like to come," said Cassandra.

Apart from wishing to please Mrs Turner, it was right to be harrowed by such an occasion. It would be like her last day at school all over again.

"Thank you, Alma," said Mrs Turner, taking her prayer-book from the head girl, who waited outside her door and followed her into the hall. Cassandra stayed at the back, feeling that there was no especial place for her there any more, except to Mrs Turner, whose love was none the less for being manifested in commonplace ways, who approved of human-nature, reserving intolerance for the truly intolerable.

Cassandra looked about her, hoping to experience nostalgia, at the English mistress, with her head on one side and neck flushed, singing furiously; at Mademoiselle with her moustache growing more emphasised with the years; at the reproduction of Saint Francis and the Birds—a threadbare little picture. This evening, there was no Charity Chapter or "O God Our Help" to play delightfully upon her nerves, merely half a dozen verses of Old Testament genealogy and a commonplace hymn, much open to girlish parody, "O For a Faith That Will Not Shrink."

'The trouble is,' she thought, 'that I am dead and indifferent to all this, grown out of it and ready for something new. The opportunity for emotion comes when the emotion is dead.'

"A faith that keeps the narrow way. Cassie Dashwood's at the back," sang one prefect to another.

"Coming to be on the staff maybe," Alma replied, her eyes fixed innocently on her hymn-book.

"She's going to be a governess somewhere."

"What a corny sort of job—Amen," sang Alma, who went a great deal to the cinema in the holidays.

'How young the prefects look!' Cassandra was thinking. 'They are only children.' When she had come here first as a little girl, they had seemed women to her, some of them with their hair up—Helen Turner herself, with plaited circles clapped over her ears, one of the ugliest of hair fashions. But it had given them a look of maturity, which none of the girls had now.

"Amen," warbled the English mistress, closing her eyes at the same time as her hymn-book; her singing done, the red subsided at her neck. Mademoiselle, it was understood, was there to help keep order, not to assist in the Protestant devotions. She stood with her hands folded on her abdomen, looking as if she were waiting for them to finish.

Mrs Turner went down heavily on her embroidered hassock and began to pray. One of the prefects leant forward and poked with her hymn-book at two juniors whose plaits hung closely together as they whispered.

Mademoiselle made a sort of shelter for her eyes with one hand, but rather as if to rest herself from the glare of the lights than to commune with her maker.

"And strengthen, O Lord," ordered Mrs Turner, "those who are going out from our midst into the world. Keep them from all harm and deliver them from temptation."

When Mrs Turner had dismissed the girls to their beds and said good night to the mistress on duty, she took Cassandra back to her sitting-room, where two glasses of Benger's had been placed on a tray by the fire.

"I think I shall write to Margaret to ask her to give you a good look-over when you get there," she said, as she warmed her legs by the fire and began to sip. "I have no prejudice at all against women doctors. Especially dear Margaret, whom I have known since . . . dear, I hope you don't dislike that very much. Ah, good, then drink it up and it will help you to sleep."

"But I always do sleep very well," said Cassandra.

"And so you should, dear, at your age. Why, it would be a very strange thing if you did not. . . . No, don't move, it is just a hairpin, and here it is! They slip into the loose-covers, and here is a penny as well . . . and some crumbs, I'm afraid . . . I must speak to Ethel. She is not always . . ."

"Won't you tell me something about the Vanbrughs?" Cassandra asked. She was not interrupting, for Mrs Turner had stopped speaking while she searched.

"I can tell you nothing," she said. "Of course, I knew Margaret—but none of the others. I believe I met her mother once, but nothing remains of that but a picture of her red hat, which I thought unsuitable on such a pale lady, apart from disliking all red hats very much indeed always . . . but that is not helpful to you. . . . I believe she is delicate. . . . She was very pale . . . unless she has improved in health, which I hope very much. The little girl I have never met, nor indeed her father, and why she mayn't go to school like other children, I can't imagine . . . it is the forming of character, which contact with other girls would . . . so much more important than . . . no governess can give that . . . but it will fill in an awkward little time for you." She dabbed at her milky upper lip with a crumpled handkerchief and began to shuffle

12

through some papers on the table beside her. "There was the letter I had from Margaret." She stood up and took a sheaf of envelopes from the mirror. . . . "Oh, here is the little snap of Helen's boy . . ."

Cassandra sat holding the photograph of a fat baby and waited expectantly.

"No, it seems not to be here. I kept it, that I do know . . . for it was a little puzzling to me at first. 'My cousin, Marion,' Margaret wrote, 'is looking for someone to teach his little girl.' '*His!*' I thought, '*Marion! His!*' But I discovered that it was one of those names like Evelyn or Hilary or Lindsay that can be either. With an 'o', you see. But 'o' or not, I think it rather girlish for a grown man. No, the letter has completely vanished . . . it is most odd. Isn't he simply a darling . . . and so like Helen at that age . . ." Mrs Turner took up a large speckled sock and began to turn its heel. "I shall knit for half-an-hour, I think, but if I were you I should have an early night . . . to-morrow there will be so much . . . such a long way . . . I will get Ethel to call you in time, with a cup of tea . . . that will start you off well. I shall see you at breakfast."

So, dismissed and without hope of further information about her future employer, Cassandra stood up. She would have liked to have said 'Dear Mrs Turner!', to have made some impulsive and affectionate gesture, but Mrs Turner knitted calmly, her hair collapsing on her shoulder and dropping tortoiseshell pins into her lap. She lifted her cheek and Cassandra kissed her good night, feeling like her daughter. "Good night, Mrs Turner."

"Good night, Cassandra. Always know this is your home, dear. I asked Ethel to put a hot bottle in your bed, but mind your toes on it, for it is one of those nasty stone ones and I shouldn't like you to hurt yourself. You can find your way, dear, can't you?"

Cassandra crossed the hall, which was dark and glassy. She met no one on her way upstairs. Her room was furnished with odds and ends, an unravelling wicker chair, a bamboo table with a Bible and a jug of lemonade almost solid with pieces of cut-up fruit, an iron bedstead and a thin honeycomb quilt. She opened the window and looked at the playing-field and the tossing plumes of poplars at the far end. She began to think of the past, methodically, as if she could find a phrase to sum-up, to carry with her to-morrow into the future; but the wind had sprung up rather boisterously and the curtains flapped and wound themselves round her. She disentangled herself and began to undress. 'Marion Vanbrugh is not a name that promises well,' she thought, as she got into bed and struck her toes upon the stone bottle.

.　　　.　　　.　　　.　　　.

Downstairs, Mrs Turner laid down her speckly knitting and lit a cigarette in a rather amateurish way. From the bookcase she took a little mottled volume vaguely entitled *The Classical Tradition*, which she had written years ago, enriching herself to the extent of eight pounds. On the fly-leaf she wrote in red ink 'To Cassandra Dashwood, with love from Lucy Turner.' Then she wiped her fingers on a piece of blotting-paper and puffed a little more at her cigarette. 'Dear Cassandra,' she sighed. She was a fundamentally optimistic woman and was perfectly prepared for her little book to go a long way to changing some of Cassandra's melancholy and romantic notions about life, and substituting in their stead, perhaps, that cool and truthful regard which she herself so deeply admired. "To see life steadily and see it whole," she murmured, putting the little present where she would be sure to find it in the morning. The cigarette was too much for her; she was tired of waving away the smoke. She threw it on the fire.

14

CHAPTER TWO

THE WET FIELDS were dealt out one after another for Cassandra's benefit. She sat with her back to the engine (as Mrs Turner had seen her off), with *The Classical Tradition* and a pile of sandwiches wrapped in a stiff damask napkin on her lap. Sodden cattle stood facing north, or hunched under hedges in the drizzle. The train ripped through the sullen landscape like scissors through calico; each time it veered round westwards rain hit the window in long slashes. ' Is it time we move through or space? ' Cassandra wondered, lulled by the sequence of the English landscape—the backs of houses and sheds, fields, a canal with barges, brickworks, plantations, the little lane going down under the bridge, fields, the backs of houses. Then the wet blackness of stations, sidings, the jagged edge of shelters beneath which people stood bleakly with luggage, and sometimes children, awaiting trains.

The Classical Tradition had a strange fungus smell and its pages were stippled with moles. The prose was formal and exact, remote from Mrs Turner's personality and yielding up nothing between the lines, so Cassandra clicked open her little case and brought out *The Woman in White*.

Behind the cover of the book, she smuggled up her egg sandwiches and began to eat, secretly and without enjoyment, her fingers searching furtively in the table napkin, the printed page guarding her shyness. The other people in the compartment eyed her in a drowsy, dully baleful way, jogging on, lulled into blankness of mind by the rocking of the train, anæsthetised almost by the rain and the darkening afternoon and the train's rhythm; each wrapped away separately in a cocoon woven of vague dreaming and reflection.

Cassandra folded up the last two sandwiches, brushed some crumbs of egg-yolk off her skirt and began to look out of the window again.

The train was winding its way through water-meadows, and had begun to slow up as the landscape grew lusher and wetter, as if oppressed by the moisture-laden hedges and low, swollen clouds. The plump woman opposite Cassandra smoothed on her gloves, cleared a little space on the misty glass with her cuff, peered out, sank back, holding her ticket ready, yawning repeatedly.

"Oh, I'm yawning," she said, catching Cassandra's glance, patting her mouth with her fist, her eyes watering. "Tiring weather."

Cassandra agreed, feeling ill at ease, vaguely suspicious of the blonde ripeness of the woman, embarrassed by her, as the young are embarrassed at being singled out by their elders.

"You going far?"

"To Cropthorne."

"Fancy that!"

Cassandra, too, cleared a little peephole and glanced out.

"Got friends there, in the village?"

"No, I'm going to Cropthorne Manor—as a governess," Cassandra said wretchedly.

The others, she knew, were leaning back easily, listening, watching through half-closed eyes.

"Governess, eh? So that's the latest, is it? Anyone meeting you? If not, come in and have a cup of tea on your way. I'm at the pub down the hill from the Manor. You're very welcome."

"I think someone is meeting me in a car."

"That'll be Margaret, then. Well, another time, perhaps." She had a way of settling her blue fox across her

16

breast and smiling down with pleasure and approval—it might equally well have been pleasure at the fur or the bosom, since both were magnificent. A dusky, pleasant perfume came from her as she stirred, and the little charms hanging from her bracelet jingled softly. "Tom's a nice boy," she went on. "Margaret's brother, that is. He's in most nights. But we never see his lordship." She winked.

Since her employer was not titled, Cassandra supposed the reference was one of contempt.

"Governess, eh!" the woman repeated, smiling comfortingly.

The word had not seemed old-fashioned to Cassandra before. For the first time, she took a glance from outside at all it might imply. She was setting out with nothing to commend her to such a profession, beyond the fact of her school lessons being fresh still in her mind and, along with that, a very proper willingness to fall in love, the more despairingly the better, with her employer.

"Nearly there," said the woman, leaning forward. Cassandra trembled a little as she put away her book, searched for her ticket.

"Look!" The woman tapped her on the knee, pointed out of the steamy glass. "Oh, it's gone. Never mind. You'll see plenty of it before long. All too soon be glad to get away from it, I don't doubt."

Cassandra had caught only a fleeting glimpse of grey walls among trees and now could see a broad stream lying in the meadows, unmoving, thick with weeds.

As the train slowed under the spiked edge of the platform shelter only Cassandra and the woman in the blue fox stirred. The others did no more than move their eyes a little to watch them leaving the compartment.

"How is she supposed to know you?" the woman asked, wrenching open the door. "You should have worn a red carnation or something of that sort." To herself she thought : ' She'll know you all right.'

Cassandra had begun to wonder the same thing, astonished that Mrs Turner, who had made all the arrangements, done all the letter-writing, could have overlooked so important a detail.

After all, there were not so many people on the platform to choose from. If Cassandra stood out a mile, as her travelling companion had thought, so did Margaret, waiting beside the ticket collector. She was bare-headed, with frizzy dark hair drawn into a bun at the back; her face was pale, her lips uncoloured. Of course, there had been no necessity to worry, for the woman swept Cassandra in front of her along the platform.

"Mrs Osborne ! "

Margaret had seen, but, nevertheless, gave a little start. "Mrs Veal. Good afternoon. I am ..."

"Here she is. Now, what an arrangement. How would you have gone on if I hadn't been here? No red carnations, I was just saying, or copy of *The Times* in the left hand turned back at the financial news. I should have liked to have seen two people meeting like that, after reading about it so much when I was a girl."

"How do you do. I expect you are Miss Dashwood. I am Dr Osborne. Mr Vanbrugh's cousin."

Cassandra shifted her case to the left hand and took Margaret's. "Have you your ticket?"

"Oh, yes ! " She put her case down and went through her pockets.

"Can I take you to the bottom of the hill?" Margaret asked Mrs Veal.

"Well, that would be nice. I certainly won't say ' no '."

They passed through the gangway, and Margaret walked slightly ahead of them to the car in the station yard.

"I am in luck's way," Mrs Veal said now and again as they drove down the village street, a long piece of ribbon-building with a couple of shops and three or four chapels, ugly in various ways.

Mrs Veal sat in the back, leaning forward, so that her perfume reached them in little drifts each time she moved.

"*Not* a very picturesque village," she observed. "But you'll grow to be very fond of it. That I do know. Dead-alive hole I once thought it. Well, it doesn't *look* much—especially this weather."

Margaret's hair was frosted all over with the fine moisture, her tweeds, too. She drove, with her head a little on one side, her elbow resting on the car window, her large white hands very loose on the steering wheel.

"Here we are, then. What about a cup of tea?" asked Mrs Veal, as the car slushed into soft gravel in front of a pub. The pub had its door shut. The signboard—or rather piece of tin stamped with a brewery trade-mark—swung on a sort of gallows near the road. "The Blacksmith's Arms".

"Well, no. I think my mother will keep tea for us at home," Margaret was saying.

Mrs Veal got together her bag and gloves and parcels and stepped out of the car backwards. "*Au revoir*, then. Thanks so much."

"Good-bye," said Margaret, and then, to Cassandra as she brought the car on to the road again, "I hope she wasn't an annoyance to you on your journey. She has a heart of gold," she added unkindly.

Cassandra murmured.

The car slowed and turned off the road into a drive, between gateposts and broken gryphons, past a mouldering lodge where some bits of washing hung limply in the drizzle. They went curving through laurels to the house. Cassandra somehow—while getting out of the car, managing her

19

belongings, and following Margaret—received an impression of the façade and, as well as the rows of sashed windows and not quite central pediment, smaller details were snatched at and relinquished again by her commenting eye; pieces of dismembered statuary, of dark grey stucco fallen from the walls and a wrought-iron lamp at the head of the steps with its greenish glass cracked.

The front door was open and rain had entered the hall.

"I don't know what you are going to make of Sophy," Margaret said, as they crossed—Cassandra tip-toeing almost —the black and white tiles. Her tone was cold and unpromising, as if she thought 'Rather you than I!' But Cassandra had grown up in the dark shadow of her father's moral courage and could not be daunted so easily or, if daunted, would not show as much or give in.

"*We* make nothing of her," Margaret added, as she opened a door. Then, thinking Cassandra looked stricken, she suddenly put her arm across the girl's back and patted her shoulder in a clumsy, prefectish gesture. Cassandra felt that she would be embarrassed at any moment by some phrase of old-fashioned slang out of Angela Brazil, but Margaret led her forward and introduced her to a spiderish lady sitting by the fire eating a piece of Ryvita.

"This is Miss Dashwood, mother. My mother, Mrs Vanbrugh. Where is Sophy?"

"How do you do, dear. She had some tea and went to her father for her Latin lesson." Mrs Vanbrugh brushed crumbs off her skirt into the hearth.

Margaret laid her hands on the sides of the teapot. "Oh, mother, let's have some *fresh*. I'll take Miss Dashwood upstairs, but I truly am dying for tea."

"You ask Nanny then, dear. I hardly like to."

"Oh, God!"

Once more they crossed the hall with its oppressive smell

of damp stone. Cassandra never allowed herself to have feelings when she was in the company of other people. She was too young to permit herself any forebodings as she followed Margaret upstairs. She was waiting until she should be alone to decide what sort of impression had been made upon her by the toppling statuary without, and faded damask, cobwebs, dusty cornices and unpeeling wallpaper within.

A gallery ran round the hall, giving opportunities for a mad sort of architecture, as if the upper part of the house had been planned solely for games of hide-and-seek, for evasions and sudden encounters. Rooms and landings lay at different levels and staircases ran off to right and left, some ascending, some burrowing down again.

Margaret could not merely open a door; she flung it open, and then, what was more, crossed the room in front of Cassandra and flung open the windows one after another, as if hoping to dilute the mouldy ancient smell of the place. She explained about the bathroom (" down the little staircase on your left and then across the half-landing and under the archway on the right "), so that Cassandra could never have followed the instructions, and then she said " I shall see about the tea," and left her to confront her own small label-plastered trunk (for her father had visited come cultural centre every summer holiday), and to inspect the Edwardian bed of brass and pleated silk.

She crossed the threadbare, pink-wreathed carpet and looked out of the window, learning her new limits, like a prisoner going for the first time into his cell. Below her, outside, a goose wandered through the ruins of an old rose garden, walking between the weeds with a sedate air.

" What are you looking at?"

A little girl leaned against the door, looking in from the dark landing.

"Are you Sophy?"

"Yes. What were you looking at?"

As Cassandra came towards her, so that she could see more plainly the child's pale, violin-shaped face, a door opened suddenly downstairs, releasing the sound of voices in angry dissent, voices which separated, echoed across the hall and, finally, trailed away.

When Margaret came upstairs, Cassandra was standing beside Sophy in the doorway. They had looked at one another, but scarcely spoken.

Margaret's forehead was flushed, but whether from anger or the stairs it was not easy to say.

"The tea is ready," she called.

She paused with her hand on the bannister and looked up at them.

"Ah, there you are, Sophy. Bring Miss Dashwood down for some tea. Where is Marion? Where is your father?"

"The neuralgia came again."

Margaret gave a sharp sigh. "Come along, then!" She disappeared down the stairs as if she could not wait longer for her tea.

"Come along, then," Sophy echoed.

CHAPTER THREE

"If you discover anything muttering in dark corners, it is Nanny and you must not mind her," said Margaret.

"Hush dear," said the oldish lady, still sitting among the Ryvita crumbs.

"She wasn't muttering at you just now," Sophy pointed out.

"How did your Latin lesson go, dear?"

Sophy shrugged. "It has gone," she said simply.

"And your daddy has toothache?"

Margaret laughed with pleasure.

"A perfectly civil question," said her mother.

"Marion does not merely have toothache."

"I thought it was toothache ... that was all ..."

"Of course it is toothache."

"And he won't be called 'Daddy'," said Sophy.

"He is your father, isn't he? Surely ..."

Margaret said: "Truth is stranger than fiction." It was only *just* said, as she took up a filled cup and passed it to Cassandra. "Don't *you* think truth is stranger than fiction, Miss Dashwood?" Her tone was engaging, artificial.

"I think we have to believe things that happen in real life, which we could not believe in a book," said Cassandra, who didn't know what she was being asked.

"Exactly what I meant," Margaret said quietly.

"Take a spoonful of Bemax on that," said her mother.

"On what? Me? Oh, Sophy! Sophy, eat your Bemax or mushrooms will grow inside you."

Sophy imagined thick shelves of fungus branching out from her ribs, and sprinkled Bemax on her jam.

23

" You are having two teas."

" Yes, Aunt Tinty."

" What about you, Miss Dashwood? "

Margaret offered a little dish.

" Oh, no, thank you." Then Cassandra blushed, feeling the child's eyes on her, to see how she would take the teasing.

" I think Sophy should show you round," Margaret suggested. " Then you will get to know one another."

" But Miss Dashwood is tired. Sitting in a train is so very fatiguing."

" No, I should like to do that, if Sophy would like it, too."

They all thought she was not starting off as she must go on. Sophy's expression, as she stood up, meant obviously that whether she liked it or not had no significance.

" Well, it will be a breath of fresh air," said Aunt Tinty, with all the reverence of an indoor sort of person for the open air.

" She is prim," said Margaret, when she was alone with her mother.

" No. She is shy. And she is young. You should not speak harshly of Marion in front of her. After all, you live here . . ."

" No, I am staying here . . . there is a difference."

" If you are a guest then your sarcasm is all the more awkward."

" How can I be a guest when I pay him thirty-five shillings a week? "

" And, then, he *is* her employer. If she cannot respect him it will be very wretched for all of us."

" We are in for a thin time, then," said her daughter.

.   .   .   .   .

" Indoors or out? " Sophy asked sullenly, out in the hall. She put her arms out stiffly from her body and spun round;

24

then as if that had been her last spurt of energy, she flagged suddenly, cast herself down on a settle and began to chew the end of a pigtail.

" Indoors first," said Cassandra, knowing she must take a strong line. " Then," she continued, " if it has stopped raining and we are not too tired, we can walk round the garden."

The eyes measured her, the pigtail was flipped back over a shoulder and the child jerked herself to her feet. " Come on then," she said ungraciously, and they began their tour of the vast, decaying place which was an examination of one another rather than an inspection of the house.

" The library!" Sophy began, standing with her back to the opened door, displaying the rows of calf and gilt. "There is a priest's-hole in the side of the fireplace," she added, as if she had done this job before. She even led the way forward, but the smell of dampish soot repelled her. Cassandra took down a book and glanced through it, which, on account of her upbringing, she could not help doing.

> " Awake therefore that gentle paffion in every fwain: for, lo! adorned with all the charms in which Nature can array her; bedecked with beauty, youth, fprightlinefs, innocence, modefty and tendernefs breathing fweetnefs from her rofy lips, and darting brightnefs from her fparkling eyes . . ."

" Those books smell horrible," said Sophy.

Cassandra raised it to her face. " It's a sweet, dusty smell."

" It turns my stomach over," said Sophy. " Like going to church."

Cassandra put the book back and followed Sophy along the corridors and up little staircases. Sometimes the child opened doors and made announcements. They came to the schoolroom, which was no cosy, shabby place with fireguard and cuckoo-clock. Cassandra could find nothing there more childish than an exercise book and *Caesar's Gallic War*

25

lying on the table. She fluttered the pages as Sophy went to the window, and was a little relieved to see Caesar's profile made less austere by inked-in spectacles and moustache.

" It is only a cat," Sophy was saying, bowed secretively over something on the window-seat. " It is only an ill cat."

" Your cat?"

The creature sneezed and Cassandra came to see. The little black face ran with tears, the creamy fur on the back clung together, as if with sweat. " A Siamese?"

Sophy said nothing, swung a foot carelessly, looked out of the window.

" It is only a kitten," said Cassandra.

Then with sudden anguish, Sophy asked: " I think it is dying?" And her voice wavered and dropped, and she turned to the window again.

Cassandra knelt by the cat's basket, took up one of the silky black legs. The unfocused, blurred gentian eyes were lifted towards her and all the time the tears ran on to its little pink tongue.

" It means all the more to me, because my mother gave it to me—on the day I was confirmed," Sophy went on.

" But your mother died many years ago," Cassandra said, as gently as she could, although she was determined to show herself not gullible. " When you were too little to remember."

" All the same she gave it me," the child said stubbornly, looking desperately affronted.

" The point is," Cassandra said, " we need some help for him."

" She is a lady cat," said Sophy, with great dignity.

" Your father, does he know?"

" No."

" Then he must be told. These cats are often valuable."

26

"They have royal blood," Sophy agreed. "*I* must cure her, though," she went on, with a change of voice. "If my father did, she would stop being my cat—and she *is* mine—even if she dies, she is still mine."

"Mothers with ill children have doctors. That doesn't make the children less their own. What about your Aunt Margaret?"

"She is a human-being doctor, not a vet. And she is only a sort of half-cousin to me, anyhow. Not an aunt."

"She might help."

"*You* cure her," Sophy said all at once and, again, it seemed as if she had used her last little bit of energy.

Cassandra was aware of all she had been asked to do and what it meant to the child to place the responsibility of life and death upon another's shoulders.

"Let's coax her with some warm milk," she began at once. "And a little glucose, if there is any."

"Oh, glucose! My Aunt Tinty sprinkles that on everything. There is always a bowlful in the sideboard. It restores vitality."

"Then that seems to be just the thing we need."

At the door, Sophy turned and said: "Eight days is the longest a cat can go without food, and she has already been three."

"It will be all right." Cassandra felt pity, too, watching the cat's tear-furrowed head turning so aloofly; for it is a sickening thing to bear, seeing the proud laid low, or elegance overthrown. She waited in the cold room, stroking the kitten's suede-padded paw. Outside, the sky, above a cobbled courtyard, congealed into darkness. Once Sophy's footsteps had sped away, no sound came from the house, but still she could not let herself face her depression which, once indulged in, might not be put easily away should anybody come. Someone did come.

27

A man with a trilby hat forgotten on the back of his head, like some American newspaper man in a film, slouched into the room and stopped. He did not remove his hat, but he said with an assumed Colonial accent: " Well, I guess it must be our Miss Dashwood."

She released the cat's paw and stood up. "How do you do."

" *And* how do *you* do ? " As she put out her hand to be wrung, she met a powerful smell of alcohol.

" Where's Sophy ? "

" She's gone to fetch some milk for the cat."

" Milk for the cat." He seemed to turn the idea over in his mind, then he nodded. " Well, we'll be having some little talks," he said, rocking back and forth on his heels. " But I must be off now. Make yourself comfortable." He glanced round the cheerless room, his hopefulness faltered, and he said good-bye and disappeared.

When Sophy came back, her head bent over the dish of swinging milk, Cassandra said, unsure of herself : " Your father looked in."

Sophy stopped, seeming puzzled. " I doubt it," she said.

" Perhaps it wasn't your father," Cassandra suggested hopefully.

" Did he smell of wine ? "

" Of course not," Cassandra said truthfully, although she thought she was telling a necessary lie.

" Did he wear a hat, then ? "

" Yes, he wore a hat."

" Then that was Tom, my cousin Tom. He's not the least bit like my father." She set the milk down on the window-sill. " And he must've smelt of wine," she said finally.

The cat turned her head fastidiously from the milk, looked out of the window as if offended.

" You see ! " said Sophy, tragically.

.   .   .   .

Sophy went to bed before supper. She said her prayers facing a photograph of her mother, as if it were a graven image. Cassandra, fidgeting round the room, a little embarrassed, thought the photograph itself unsuitable for such a purpose, the secretly smiling face, the mocking, insolent eyes.

At supper there were only the three women, but Margaret indicated a folded white note on Cassandra's plate.

" My cousin wrote it for you when I took his tablets to him."

" You know, Margaret," said Aunt Tinty, " I wouldn't wonder if it isn't migraine Marion suffers from." She took cauliflower cheese from a silver dish. The cheese had seethed and bubbled and was a curdled mass.

Cassandra unfolded the paper. A spiky, but beautiful handwriting, very black ink.

" MY DEAR MISS DASHWOOD,

Will you forgive my absence on your arrival. My cousin will have explained. I shall look forward to seeing you and welcoming you to-morrow.

MARION VANBRUGH."

Cassandra scarcely read it, but fingered it occasionally, waiting to savour it in solitude ; for it had a fine measure of importance, this first note, and the crossing of every ' t ', the flying comma, each linked letter must be analysed for its clue.

" Forgive my mentioning my own private affairs," said Margaret casually, " but I find, mother, that I am expecting a child."

The old woman started, her fork jagged across her plate. " Why, Margaret, what a way to say such a thing ! What a way to tell your mother such a thing ! In the middle of a meal."

" It was the way I preferred," Margaret said cruelly.

Cassandra realised that she had been waited for, to be used as a screen by Margaret against her mother's fussing.

She flushed, because she resented being put to this use, hated the other's rudeness.

"In the circumstances, I shall prolong my holiday. Ben would rather I did that. Dobby must manage."

Ben was her husband, Dobby her partner. This was not explained to Cassandra.

"But will Marion like it?" Tinty began, but fearing lest her daughter might say, in front of the governess, "he will like the money," or something embarrassing and impossible of that kind, she went on quickly: "Well, it will be very nice, I dare say. That is good news your first evening with us, Miss Dashwood. You must forgive our discussing these things, but we have so little time together."

Indeed, they only had all day.

"Someone has been at the glucose," Tinty went on, spooning it over her stewed apple. "It was scattered all over the sideboard."

Cassandra blushed. Margaret noted the blush.

"Did you go round the garden with Sophy?" Tinty asked.

"No. It went on raining."

"So it did. What a pity! It would have given you an appetite."

"Nothing could give her an appetite for this," said Margaret, pushing aside the mush of apple.

"No, it isn't very nice," her mother agreed. "Never mind."

After supper, they sat for a while in the drawing-room, and Margaret strummed a little at the piano and then jumped up and went restlessly to the long windows at the front of the house. She looked out at the rainy garden, beating her knuckles on the glass softly, and Cassandra saw her face quieter and relaxed, her expression peaceful. Aunt Tinty wrote a long letter to a distant relation, exposing it, bit by bit as it was written, to Margaret's bullying comments.

Soon Cassandra said good night and went upstairs. As she

passed the room which Sophy had whispered was her father's, she heard footsteps going up and down over a carpeted floor. She went on down the corridor, through archways, round corners, and came to her own room.

On the dressing-table she disposed her parents' photographs, her mother's ivory and initialled brushes; her few books she stacked on the bedside table; hung up her clothes in a tremendous wardrobe above a pair of old boot-trees. She went to the window and leant out for a moment. The goose wandered no more in the rose garden. Rain fell from leaf to leaf, rolled down the ivy, ran over the windows, oily like gin. She turned away and began to undress, brushed out her smooth brown hair a hundred times as her mother had always said she should and then (her father's bidding) read a page of Shakespeare, peering at the thin India paper with her rather weak eyes; and, reaching the bottom of the page and leaving Lady Macbeth in the middle of unsexing herself, she closed the book and climbed into the frivolous Edwardian bed.

Now, at last, the luxury might for a little be indulged in— the summing-up, the verdict, the easy weeping, the pity. She cried a little against her arm, the tears running out of the corners of her eyes, until she was forced to stop so that she might strain her ears listening to a muffled commotion somewhere outside, a scuffling on loose wet gravel, a gentle cursing. The noise stopped abruptly and a door slammed. Rather fearfully, for it was all unlike the atmosphere of home or school or any she had ever known, she put her head down upon the pillow and lay there, not relaxed enough now for weeping, but very tired, and soon, her head still filled with muddled conjecture, the boundaries grew vague, all that was familiar melted away and the fantastic, the forbidden, the gigantic stood in view; lost thoughts slipped through the majestic visions; her will loosened, she sank down through

31

sleep, losing herself, finding herself ; yet, however lost, the sleeping are unlike the dead, for still the mind murmured ' I.' She said ' I, Cassandra.' ' I, myself, Cassandra.' Then the lady in the blue fox leant forward very close and rapped on the carriage window, she smiled and drummed her knuckles hard against the glass.

At that moment, there *was* a sound like that in the house, although Cassandra did not know. It was Tom coming up the stairs and trailing his stick along the bannister-rails.

"Tom ! " hissed Margaret, coming out on to the landing, with her dressing-gown tied tightly round.

He took no notice. He walked on to his own room and slammed the door. Margaret watched for a moment and went back to bed.

In his room, Tom sat on the edge of his bed and rested his elbows on his knees and stared intently at his swinging hands. When he was tired of doing that, he began to pull at his tie; the knot slid tighter, and he cursed. After that, he sat down again for a while and rested. Presently he was altogether undressed. He poured a glass of water and placed it beside his bed, put on his pyjama jacket and suddenly, aloud, said : " O.K. Good. Swell. Fine." He felt all right, except for his head, which seemed to be opening and shutting or, like swing doors, letting in gusts of sound, long waves of quiet, gusts of sound, alternately, with regularity. He got into bed and took a sip of water. When he put his face to the pillow, lying sideways, ' the best moment of the day,' he thought. But the bed swung round suddenly and cruelly, that relentless lurching movement that gave the feeling of helpless terror in the abdomen. ' Steady,' he thought. ' Not again. Better in the morning.'

He lay very still and quiet, not to frighten sleep away, as if it would creep up stealthily, a timid little animal, would not come if it knew he was there, waiting, greedily, artfully.

32

CHAPTER FOUR

In the morning, the garden, the house, sprang up, jewelled in the bright air. Each leaf, each blade of grass flashed with colour, the broken statues of nymphs before the house whitened in the sun. Pomona and Flora, still with wet eye-sockets, wet folds of drapery, held out chipped fruit and flowers to dry.

At breakfast, there was another note beside Cassandra's plate.

" Dear Miss Dashwood,
   Will you be good enough to make out a timetable for Sophy's lessons and bring it to my room at eleven?
                                                            M.V."

Cassandra refolded the paper and was trembling a little. Aunt Tinty distributed her patent foods and watched Margaret intently. Margaret ate well and showed no signs of sickness.

After breakfast, in the schoolroom, which the sun would not reach much before Sophy's bedtime, they sat at the inky table and ruled lines on a large sheet of paper, headed it with the days of the week, and paused.

In her basket, the cat snuffled. She seemed neither better nor worse, but ate nothing and scorned her milk.

" History," Cassandra began. " What have you done?"

" Oh, I had gone all through it once and got to Elizabeth for the second time," said Sophy airily.

" Arithmetic?"

" I was just doing those sums where there are figures on top of a line and some more underneath."

" Fractions?"

" No, I don't think that was the name."

" Do you know all your tables? "

" I did once."

" Well . . . it looks like arithmetic every day. French? "
The child shrugged.

" I can read *Les Malheurs de Sophie*. I had it for my
birthday."

" Do you know any verbs? "

" Yes, I think I *do*."

" Write out the present tense of ' être '. Can you do that? "

" Yes."

She dipped her pen in the ink, considered, and wrote slanting across the page:

> " j'êtres
>
>   tu êtres
>
>   il être
>
>   nous êtrons
>
>   vous êtrez
>
>   ils . . ."

" All right! " Cassandra interrupted. " I think French
every day, too. It was a gallant try, though," she added.

At one minute to eleven, she left Sophy to learn verbs by
herself and set off along the corridor with the time-table.
Lifts rose and fell in her stomach as she knocked, and when
she heard the voice on the other side she opened the door
and stepped out of the sunlit corridor into what seemed
like darkness. She closed the door behind her and stood very
still to get her bearings, and because she trembled violently.

Strips of light and shadow slanted over the walls of the
long room; at all the windows venetian blinds were drawn.
In the barred and chequered light only details stood out;
white candles on a table, and flowers, scrolls of gilt on mirrors
and furniture, and the light that filtered in was greenish,
so that the ceiling had a green pallor and the marble fireplace

reflected green and the man who leant his elbow on the mantelpiece had the same greenish tinge upon his face and hands.

He came forward and greeted Cassandra and as she moved across the room towards him she grew accustomed to the shadows and glad of them.

"You are trembling. Why?" he asked, as he took the sheet of paper from her. "Come and sit down by the fire."

He drew up a chair opposite her and lifted an earthenware coffee-pot from the hearth and began to fill cups on a tray beside him. He handed her coffee and a cigarette and behind her little smoke-screen she could watch him studying the time-table, observed his thin face, his exaggeratedly long hands like the hands in an Elizabethan portrait, the greenish-gold hair, his rather affected clothes. She was hollowed by the fear of his cold, dissecting glance, the probability of calm sarcasm, of utter ruthlessness in conversation. He laid the paper aside without comment, as if it bored him, then leant back in his chair and laced his fingers together.

"How are you going to get on with Sophy?" he asked.

"I hope . . . I think . . . I shall do my . . ." she began to falter, in a little governessy voice.

She knew that Jane Eyre had answered up better than that to her Mr Rochester. She looked into her empty coffee cup in panic and then, fearing lest he might take it as a hint, jerked up her chin and tried to glance at him. His voice, so far, had been gentle and even and his manner patient.

"You have met my aunt who housekeeps for me. This is her home, but my cousin, her daughter, is here on a visit. She will be leaving soon."

Cassandra felt less able to speak than ever.

"There is no period for Latin on the time-table," he observed smoothly.

"I thought . . . She knows scarcely any French yet."

" Latin is more important than French. Do you read Greek, Miss Dashwood?"

" No."

"No, well, I shall take Sophy for Greek myself then. Perhaps in the afternoon ..."

" She is a little young . . . surely?"

" Her mother was reading Homer in the original at the age of eight." He drank some coffee, but he still watched her. Cassandra thought, to comfort herself, that it is always the wonderful dead who have done all the marvels.

" Not that Sophy is much like her mother. In any way. Her looks even. Beauty like her mother's rarely reproduces itself. No, Sophy is more like her cousin, Margaret."

His features she considered ill-matched—the two halves of his face belonging, it might have been, to different men, or as if seen through a flawed mirror, like the room itself, which was cracked by the long crooked shadows and the shifting slatted light.

" When you are not looking after Sophy, what will you do?"

He leaned forward and poured more coffee into her cup. " Will you walk about in the garden with a book in your hand, which you will never read? That is all there is to do here. There is all day long and the night, too ; and yet, there is only time to dip into books and turn over a few pages. You'll find that. When there is so *much* time, there is never enough. Those long summers in the Russian novels—the endless bewitched country summers—and the idle men and women—making lace. Do you remember in *A Month in the Country*—that was how Natalia described their conversation—it was love conversation, too—that it was making lace . . . they never moved an inch to the left or right . . . only idle people are like that . . . they talk to pass the time for they know that time is only a landscape we travel

across. . . . They hope to make a busy journey of it . . ."
His fingers stroked between his eyes. ". . . I walk about my
room—this room—and about the garden, with a book in
my hand, with my finger marking the place, even, as if I
were going to read at any moment. But I seldom do.
Although I was not always idle."

"Why does Sophy tell untruths about her mother?" Cassandra asked, with the sharp edge to her voice of sudden and
undisciplined courage.

"We all tell lies about her," he said calmly.

"But Sophy could not remember her."

"You *can* remember what you have never had," he insisted.

"When did her mother die?" She said 'her mother',
since she could not say 'your wife'.

"She died in childbirth. Sophy was the child." He
watched her, then he went on: "You see, that does happen
in real life as well as in the novels. Though not as com-
monly."

"Then she . . ."

"Obviously Sophy can never have known her. *She* is
making lace, too, perhaps."

She had come a long way from the life of yesterday, of
the day before that—the shabby home, the traffic, the bush
full of tram tickets, the crowds on the pavements, clotting,
thinning out, pressing forward; travelling across time, Marion
had called it, but they were really going to work, or going
home from work, or shopping, or wooing one another.
'Quite separate,' she thought. 'Each quite separate. That
is the only safe way of looking at it. And we can never be
safe unless we believe we are great and that human life is
abiding and the sun constant and that we matter. Once
broken, that fragile illusion would disclose the secret panic,
the vacuity within us. Life then could not be tolerable.'

Marion, with his talk of lace-making, had threatened to reveal the panic and confusion and so create an intolerable world for her.

"I should get back to Sophy, perhaps."

He stood up, but ignored her remark.

"*Your* mother died too short a while ago for you to be telling lies about her either to others or yourself. It will be a strange time for you, the time between her death and the day when you begin falsifying her—only a little while since you woke to the first day without her, that first morning!" He covered his eyes with his hand, but with a gesture of fatigue not of grief. "The moment when perhaps you picked up the book she had been reading, with a letter slipped in half-way to mark her place. And took the letter out and put the book back upon the shelf in its place. But soon, out of her bones will grow the new picture of her, more beautiful, more romantic . . ." (He cut the air with his hand, which he put in his pocket, a gesture of impatience) " . . . . than ever in life, always loving, never angry, never guilty." He fell silent and stood looking down into the little gold fire, and the clock ticked heavily in the darkened rococo room.

' He will do to fall in love with,' Cassandra thought with some relief. She had never been spoken to in this way before.

"So bear with Sophy and her little lies," he said, not meaning this only. "And come and talk to me sometimes." He took her hand and then held it longer and led her to the window, where the light faltered over her as if she were beneath broken water. He released the blind and the sun fell warmly upon them. In this new light, he looked very intently at her face as if he counted her features or would draw her, seeing only the face and not minding her emotions or what she suffered under his scrutiny. She looked back, candid, without coquetry, as sometimes the young can.

"So you don't know Greek? Shall I teach you? Shall

38

we read together? And I turn into a governess for a change? How will that be? It will help to keep us both awake for a little, to resist the spell."

"Yes. I should like to learn," she said—her father's daughter.

"Good."

He stood looking out at the garden as if he had forgotten her, like a sick person whose attention wanders. She realised it was time for her to go away. When she reached the door, not knowing how to take leave, pausing uncertainly, he looked up and smiled and said: "No one shall share our lessons," meaning Sophy.

As soon as the door was closed, he drew down the blind again and stood very still with his fingers once more pressed against his eyes.

.   .   .   .   .

Tom lay in bed until eleven. The room was stuffy and untidy, but he lay there between waking and drowsing, longing for a drink. The water had gone stale, but he drank it. It seemed to wash about in him and slap the sides of his stomach, yet not quenching his thirst. 'Butterfly stomach!' he thought.

In one corner a skeleton sat up crookedly in a plush-covered chair. The room would not have been the same without old Bony, who always wore Tom's hat at night, wore it now, after Tom's own fashion, tipped to the back of the skull.

Presently Tom got up. Half-dressed, he sat down at his desk to finish the drawing he had begun the day before. The same drawings hung all round the room—the human body, finely done in sepia ink, the anatomy in perfect detail, but each picture quixotic, incongruous in some way—flesh vanishing to reveal ribs or thigh-bone, or a skeleton blossoming into flesh, one arm or a face of great beauty, eyes covered

39

with fig-leaves. This one which he did so painstakingly was like an engraving in some ancient medical book—the Rubens ripeness of the woman, the large belly laid open to show a child curled in the womb, the four lappets of flesh furled back like leaves. It was a beautiful and complicated drawing, but done on a scrap of torn paper, not clean. He placed a rose in the woman's hand, drew in the veins along one arm and the coarse hair starting from the armpit, then, looking pleased, he cleaned his pen-nib carefully and finished dressing.

.   .   .   .   .

Cassandra had gone back in a dream to release Sophy from her French verbs. As she turned a corner, she came upon an old woman sweeping some stairs. When she saw Cassandra she muttered angrily and hid her dustpan and brush behind her skirt.

"Just saw a little dust. The mess they make!"

She appeared not to like being discovered with the dustpan, so Cassandra went on and left her to her mumbling.

Sophy was kneeling at the window-seat beside her cat, dipping her fingers in a saucer of blood.

"I found this in the larder under the beef—raw blood. I thought it might tempt her appetite." She smeared some round the cat's mouth, but the poor creature moved its head back, looking piteously away and shaking the little red drops off her whiskers.

"There he goes!" Sophy leant out of the window, flicking the blood off her fingers over the sill.

Tom crossed the cobbles. He wore his hat; he went jauntily down to the pub, slipping out the back way to avoid his sister and her personal remarks about his liver. 'A nice dry Martini,' he thought. 'Or a couple.' He felt fine. Only the vaguest whisperings and creakings disturbed him, the shifting perspectives, a little uncertainty in his bowels, the little acid flutterings in his stomach. 'Otherwise, fine!' he thought. 'And a coupla dry Martinis'll put that right.'

"He sometimes turns and waves when he gets to the grapevines, but to-day he didn't," said Sophy.

.   .   .   .   .

As Tom walked towards his drink he felt grander and grander. The jewelled air smote him, he took breaths of it steadily into his soiled lungs. By the time he reached "The Blacksmith's Arms" he knew he was committed by the good fortune of his health and spirits to a long morning session of drinking.

Mrs Veal tapped his palm with her pointed red nails as she handed him his change. He tried to close on her fingers with his own, but she was too quick. She pursed her lips as if she were scandalised. She reminded him of a camel, her sandy blondeness, her curved nose and heavy eyelids, the fluffed-up hair upon her forehead.

"What are you laughing at?"

"You."

She could only feign crossness.

So the morning wore on.

CHAPTER FIVE

AFTER TWO DAYS of sitting up aloofly, the cat lost strength and lay panting, with its sides fallen in, its long brown-stockinged legs extended, its eyes covered with pus.

Suddenly Sophy lost her nerve and gave in.

" Anyone can come, if only she will get better, anyone can come."

" Fetch your father," Cassandra said.

" No, Tom."

She went like an arrow out of the room, shot forward by her own nervous tension.

It was early evening and the room looked a little brighter than it did all day. Cassandra thought the cat would not last the night. It had reached the point she had seen before in her parents' illnesses, when hope, carefully fostered, turns all at once to acceptance and indifference. It is a scarcely perceptible change, quick like the spinning of a coin; but once the coin lies flat there is no more to be done. There is a limit to our hold on life.

When Tom came he stood the cat on the table before him, looking at it closely.

" Sophy, fetch me the little attaché case from my room," he said. As soon as she had gone, he turned to Cassandra and asked : " There'll be hell to pay if this cat dies ? "

She nodded.

" As it will," he said.

He felt the cat's stomach, seemed to be concentrating on the animal, yet he went on : " Marion coddles her, wraps her in cotton-wool, Sophy, I mean. When it comes to it, she hasn't anything real to help her. No experience. I don't believe in

42

governesses, if you will excuse my saying so. I believe in going out and about, finding out things, getting the corners rubbed off." He looked at Cassandra.

"Those are vague phrases," she said.

"My cousin tries to live in the eighteenth century. Latin, and soon there's to be Greek, I hear. She wants to be rushing round with a hockey-stick, having crushes on the other girls. But there are no other girls. It's all wrong. Why should I trouble myself, be rude to you, too? Over the important things he never will stir himself. The conservatory, for instance. How many times am I to tell him, ask him? Thank you, Sophy."

He clicked open the case and took out some pills. All the time the cat was standing piteously aloof upon the table. "Hold her legs," he ordered Cassandra. The cat became possessed suddenly of a wild strength and struggled insanely. Tom held her mouth shut upon the pill, stroked under the chin, but with a convulsive madness it sought to free itself from Cassandra. Sophy ran to the wall and hid her face, screaming.

"It's done," said Tom. He laid the cat back in its basket, where it tried to lick a paw, but gave up, lay quivering and exhausted.

A long scratch ripened on Cassandra's hand, little heads of blood rose up from it. When Tom saw it, he took some antiseptic from his case and dabbed her, dealing with her in great gentleness.

"All right?"

She nodded.

"As for you, Sophy," he said sharply when he reached the door, "for God's sake, control yourself."

In the night, the cat died.

Cassandra braced herself to contend with a grief which did not come. Sophy appeared to have accepted death before it happened and was not shocked. She fell busily to preparing a funeral, planning a headstone. She laid the kitten in an old boot-box, covered it with limp ferns and went out with Cassandra to bury it. At the end of a grassy lime avenue near the house were rows of small tombstones at the foot of a round hillock.

Sophy dug the grave, while Cassandra stood by shivering and holding the cardboard coffin. The child's face, even when the earth went back over the dead animal, reflected satisfaction at a job well done, not sorrow, nor any suggestion of loss.

She brushed soil from her hands calmly.

" This little hill is a grave, too," she explained. " There is a ghost who rises from it and walks up and down this avenue, even in broad daylight. Nanny has seen it doing so. A man from the house fought a duel here early one morning and killed his friend. He was so ashamed he tried to hide the body by heaping all this earth upon it where it lay, and planting grass. One day the hill wasn't there and the next day it was."

" And how long ago was all this? " Cassandra asked drily.

" Oh, before I was born."

They walked back down the avenue towards the house. " The conservatory is out-of-bounds," Sophy said, pointing to the great ruin of dusty glass, in which a large palm tree clattered its leaves. " It isn't safe. It might come down at any time. Anyone who was inside when it happened would be cut into little shreds of flesh. So Tom said."

They skirted it widely.

" Never run round this side of the house in case you jar it," Sophy went on. " I once went inside it very gently to look at a wasp's nest, but I trembled all the time I was there—thinking of what Tom said. And when he knew I'd been in there, he lost his temper and took hold of my shoulders and

44

shook me till my teeth rattled. And then Marion came and stopped him."

"All right," said Cassandra, "but now we must get back to our lessons."

Marion's neuralgia was better. He appeared at meals, he came sometimes into the schoolroom and glanced through Sophy's books, and was to be seen in the afternoons walking in the lime avenue or sitting reading—if it was warm—on the cracked stone seat in the rose garden. 'What did he do before he was idle?' Cassandra wondered.

Between meals, the house fell under a spell. The meals brought them all together, but as soon as they were dispersed it seemed as if the rooms were all empty.

When Tom was not at the pub he lay on his bed waiting for his stomach to right itself, or, if he were able, he would sit at his littered desk drawing his strange pictures.

He lived at two levels, the life in the saloon bar; the life with the pen in his hand and the cynical, bitter, unamiable figures growing upon the endless pieces of paper—the harlot stripped of flesh but with eye-sockets coquettish above an opened fan, or the young man with his heart lying in his outstretched hand, but a heart from a medical book, with severed pipes and labelled auricles and ventricles, nothing romantic, nothing valentineish.

Margaret seemed to have established herself with or without Marion's permission. Cassandra felt towards her pregnancy a sense of both enmity and respect, which women do experience, however faintly, subtly, in the presence of fruitfulness and purpose.

Tinty, nervous and meek, bit down the thousand and one expressions of joy and looking-forward which sprang daily to her lips, held herself back from her grandmotherly planning, asked no questions, offered no glucose. Tom and Marion watched Margaret closely. Cassandra could feel at

45

mealtimes that they were narrowly observing her with fascination and distaste. Nothing was ever said.

One day at lunch Marion asked: " Is Nanny going to the cinema this afternoon?"

" Oh, I expect so, dear," said Tinty. " It's the day they change the film."

" Then Sophy may go with her."

" Is it a suitable film, though?"

" No films are suitable," said Tom, looking annoyed.

Marion ignored him. Sophy looked from one to the other.

" It's *Pride and Prejudice*," said Tinty.

Tom sniggered.

" Well that should be very nice," his mother said.

" It should be sweetly pretty," he agreed. " It should be just the thing."

" Would you like to go, Sophy?" Marion asked.

" Oh, yes. May Miss Dashwood come too?"

" Miss Dashwood and I are going to read Greek together." Cassandra blushed.

" She doesn't *know* Greek," Sophy pointed out. " I wish someone else could come. Not just Nanny and me. Tom, you come!"

" Good God, no!"

" Why not?"

" I don't want to."

" Do it because *I* want you to."

" No."

" Why not?"

" Sophy, that's enough," said Marion.

She still looked questioningly, accusingly at Tom. He gave his plate a little push, sat back in his chair and stared at her.

He did not bother to cover up the awkwardness of the moment. He sat it out.

Cassandra had a weak stomach. When she was excited or nervous or imagining herself put to a test, her bowels froze, hollowed; wings seemed to beat inside her and various large organs such as lungs and heart appeared to lose balance and plunge downwards, like a lift out of control in its shaft. The thought of the Greek lesson put her most dreadfully to the test, and the food—chocolate sago—turned acid as fast as she could eat it. She trembled—and yet a little from delight —at the prospect of sitting alone with Marion in his room, of showing herself less than intelligent, stupid even, unable to grasp simple things, unfit, therefore, to teach his daughter. Already she had been caught out, had, a day or two before, passed over a wrong gerund in Sophy's Latin and he had had to point it out when he looked through the lesson book. He had done so with kindness and courtesy, implying that she had rather overlooked the wrong than forgotten the right.

"Run and tell Nanny to pack two teas, then," said Tinty.

"Tea?" Margaret looked incredulous.

"She always takes sandwiches lest she should feel faint during the second film. Faint with hunger, I mean."

Tom clapped a handkerchief over a laugh.

"Does she have no lunch, then?" Margaret asked. "Is she so excited at the idea of the pictures that she cannot eat?"

"Shush, dear. It wouldn't be the cinema to Nanny if she had no sandwiches."

"It makes an outing of it," said Sophy, as if she alone understood.

Tom rocked in his chair.

When they saw Nanny standing in the hall in her hard black hat and carrying her American cloth bag of food, they were fearful of having laughed and a little ashamed. The light divided on the shiny straw boater as on a gramophone record. Hatpins drove into it from all sides.

"Hurry that child, for mercy's sake, miss," she called to Cassandra. "We shall be late for the Forthcoming Attractions if we don't catch the first bus."

"Speed Sophy and come when you are ready," said Marion, leaning over a banister.

Cassandra reddened again at the intimacy, as if it were his bed she was bidden to, not a Greek lesson. She worked in haste to get Sophy ready, plaited up her rather fuzzy hair, tied it with four yellow bows, handed her a handkerchief, mentioned the lavatory.

"What does 'Prejudice' mean?" Sophy struggled into her coat.

"It means a pre-conceived opinion," Cassandra replied.

"I don't think I shall enjoy it," said Sophy, wanting to back out. Unstable, she was always swinging from one desire to another, could not endure feeling compulsion, or commitment.

"Don't be silly," said Cassandra, rushing her down the stairs, from which they could see Nanny, oddly foreshortened under the wheeling lights of her hat, standing in the hall. She took Sophy with as little grace as a girl takes a young brother when she goes to meet her love. "Ah, there we are!" she said grimly, so that Cassandra could not envy Sophy her afternoon out, and turned at last, with a mingling of guilt and delight, towards Marion's room.

He was standing by one of the long windows with his hands in the pockets of his black velvet jacket. The room was white and gilt and brilliant, untidy with coloured books, not the leathery mouldy books in the library, but the bright modern books that are all gone to-morrow, God knows where. Under the warm sun the bracken in the white jar had begun to unclench its fists; above mirrors pediments were broken to make room for little gesso cherubs or scallop shells, the mirrors themselves reflecting richness.

" Did Sophy not change her mind at the last moment ? "
Marion asked.

" She was beginning to . . . I gave her no time."

" That weakness is painful, but it can't be pandered to.
She inherits it from her mother.   It must seem a trivial thing
to those who are not afflicted.   But it really can make hell for
everyone.   What does one do, I wonder ? "

" She must be made to stand by her decisions.   Then it will
become a matter of course, I daresay."

" You think that ? "   It was as if he were prepared to
believe whatever she said.   " Her mother was spoilt as a child.
We must not spoil Sophy.   In her mother, that little failing
at last assumed really distressing proportions.   At night . . .
at a party, I mean . . . she would fall in love with the whole
world, and every dull person in it, overflowing with spirits
and seeing them all reflecting her own goodness and beauty,
invite hosts of dreary people to lunch the next day."   He
took a deep breath, rather theatrically.   " Every morning,
after breakfast, as soon as the post had come, she'd sit down
by the fire accepting invitations . . . there were always so many
because she made herself pleasant to everyone, spared her
vitality in no way . . . but when the time came for her to *go*
to the party or the dance or picnic, or whatever it was, there
would be a painful *crise des nerfs*.   She would come to me
trembling, her face white. . . . ' I *can't* go.   I couldn't make
myself,' seeming like a cornered animal.   Sometimes she
would force herself to go, sick and ill as she set out, but all
would be well ; once there, she lit up, people illuminated her ;
she would come back worn out, for it had cost her something,
but always deliriously happy, committed again and again to
the same occasion.   But if she didn't go, if she gave in, then
she would mope from room to room, trailing about the house,
dead, regretful, petulant.   She had never learnt to know what
was best for her, could not have the responsibility of ordering

her own life. A terrible drawback, you know. What did you say to Sophy?"

"I think I said 'nonsense' or something like that." She could not help feeling that she had dealt too lightly with what was apparently an esteemed and reverenced family fault.

He smiled. "I think you are going to be just right for her. Are you happy?" Seeing her shyness at being asked questions about herself, he went on: "Do you like this room? It is the nicest in the house, and I keep it for myself." He began to walk about, touching books and china. "Once it was my wife's room."

'He cannot forget the dead,' she thought.

"But it is a room with a macabre little history. My great-aunt, who left this house to me, died here. She was lonely and eccentric and no servants could bear her. She lived here quite alone after her husband died. In this large house, where never a stroke of work was done or a broom put over the floors. The gardener locked her in at night and unlocked her when he came over from his cottage next morning. It all went to rack and ruin, as they say. One can imagine it. Her husband had left her a cellarful of port. So she settled down to drink it before she died. She liked this room . . . I suppose because of the sun. And I can imagine her . . . though, my God, I never came to see . . . sitting here among the cobwebs, getting drunker, eating almost nothing. The floor rotted and fell in in places, there were great holes . . . She might have broken her neck, but she never did. The gardener found her one morning, not just dead drunk, but drunk dead. Yet I suppose she died of grief and loneliness as much as anyone . . . despair and the indifference of the world."

When he was silent after speaking, it was as if he wished to reflect on his own remarks, not expecting her to do so; he did not look at her for any reaction, nor watch to see if his words had sunk in; he might have been talking to himself, a reverie on death. She guessed that the dead one was an undisputed barrier between him and life, a barrier he would never challenge, a fixed standard by which all else would inevitably fail. She felt she hated the beautiful one, the spellbinder, the child who read Homer at the age of eight, who looked out of the photograph in Sophy's room like Morgan le Fay.

"And now!" He went to the table and spread out books. "I shall teach you how to write your letters."

He felt an impatience to see her shaping them on the page, the letters with that old beauty, which seemed to him to cast a violet shadow from the sun.

'She is like a good child—curiously empty,' he decided, watching her as she took up her pen. He would have liked to have guided her hand, as if she were really a child, but brushed away the thought, leant back in his chair, rolling a cigarette, not offering her one, for she had her lesson to do. She copied the alphabet from an old primer which had 'Violet Wilding' written across it in ink faded brown. The dead again.

"Your wrist looser?" he said, lighting his cigarette. "*Psi* is like a lily."

She tried to draw the lily, made too much of it, looked up and smiled.

"This is more like the hammer and sickle," he said, turning the paper a little towards him and putting his attempt against hers.

Outside, Margaret and her mother walked up and down the terrace for a little while. Cassandra could hear the name 'Tom', first one, then the other, saying it.

After a while, Marion began to read to her in Greek, outlining in rather lame, impatient English from time to time what it was Hector was saying to his lady-wife.

51

When he closed the book, he said: "Cassandra is a beautiful name."

She waited, her heart falling against her ribs. "I should like to call you that," he said at last.

.   .   .   .   .

"I shall go up and write to Ben," Margaret was saying.

Tinty felt . . . she was sure . . . the girl meant to rest her legs. She was too proud to say: "I shall go up and lie on the bed for an hour." She was very brisk and ordinary about her pregnancy; it made no difference, she seemed to infer. Now they had finished talking about Tom—Margaret worrying her mother about him, knowing she could do nothing, had no power to stop him. It was getting worse and worse. At first (but that was years ago), when he was bored and restless, he would go down for a pint and a chat, something to do; that soon became a habit which fitted easily into his empty life. Now, it was no longer a habit, it was his purpose, the centre of him, the thing that was real, and his life must fit in with that, or he could not answer for living. Margaret said ' liver ', ' hardening arteries ', and then she said ' disgrace ' and ' bad example ' and ' God knows what people say and think '. Her mother, so timid with her, knew that was only the beginning and not important. She knew that it was Tom's mind that mattered, and his life being so empty of purpose that drink could have taken possession of the centre of him. "It was a pity he failed his exams. A pity he gave up so easily," she had said to Margaret. She even said: "His character was weak. He needed help." What she did not say, to Margaret or anyone else, although she thought it, was: "The pity was about Violet." She would never say that: even the thought did not come to her in words, not explicitly, but in a hushed sickness which had to be comforted away. Her life was made up of little anxieties which had to be

52

soothed and dispersed; as soon as one went, another came, anxieties about her son and about her own health.

She walked up and down the terrace. From Marion's window, she heard his voice speaking a strange language, words of lament, she thought, listening for a moment to the long curious vowels; words of grief and woe . . . that was the word, 'woe' . . . not of anxiety. Anxiety is the modern affliction, belonging to the long twilights, the uncertain modern weather; neither sun nor snow and neither grief nor joy. She thought of Margaret upstairs, lying with her feet up, her sailor husband torn from her at the time when she needed him. *She* seemed not to grieve, gave way to none of those long, wailing vowels; everything casual, hidden, clouded-up.

.   .   .   .   .

Margaret was hungry, not tired. She went to the kitchen. As soon as one meal was over, she began to think about the next. Food had started to entrance her.

The kitchen had its scrubbed, afternoon, waiting look. On the rocking-chair lay Nanny's film paper. Margaret took it to read while she stood in the larder eating. On the stone slab was half a gooseberry pie, caved in, and a jam-tart covered with a trellis of pastry; but she had to eat secretly what would not be missed. In the meat-safe was a slab of grey beef, overcooked, a knuckle of veal gleaming with bluish bones. Sage swung from the ceiling, brushing against a net of onions with a lisping sound; there was a brown crock full of cream cheese. She cut a thick slice of wholemeal bread, covered it with butter, then with the cheese, began to eat greedily, dealing craftily with the crumbs, turning the pages of the cinema paper. When she had finished, she was still hungry. She cut another slice and spread it as before. The thought of all this good, wholesome food going into her was pleasing. A fly from outside tried at the perforated zinc over the window. As strategy failed, it tried force. When it flew suddenly away, the silence was complete, perfect. Margaret ate more slowly, with no further sensuous delight. She felt puffed and fagged with eating. " Grossly, full of bread," she murmured, thinking she saw what it meant, felt what it meant, for the first time. And then ' crammed with distressful bread,' she remembered. Shakespeare must have been greedy too. She was sickened now by the food around her on the shelves, pulled off some bits of sage and sniffed at them— aromatic, that was better. She heard her mother calling down through the house; the voice winding thinly down the stairs, along the passages, peevishly.

Tinty had gone to see if Margaret needed anything; would have been so happy to have found her lying on the bed and wanting a cup of tea or eau-de-cologne, weeping for Ben, maybe (' Mother, you are all I have '), softened miraculously by approaching motherhood.

The bed had not been lain upon. The curtains bellied out, the only movement in the still room. So Tinty began to call and call through the house, which seemed to hold silent as if from malice.

Margaret cleared up the crumbs, smoothed over the hollow in the cheese, wiped the knife on a cloth, replaced the lid quietly on the bread-bin and crept out the back way, across the courtyard to the lime avenue, went down to sit on a grave and have a little peace, smoke a cigarette, and think of Ben, and think of the baby.

Up and down the stairs the little voice echoed petulantly, until Tom came out of his bedroom frowning and blinking and saying: " What *is* it, Mother? What the devil is lost? "

.   .   .   .   .

The afternoon blazed as they came out of the cinema. The contrast was too much. The street looked so banal after the dark where emotions grow like mushrooms, a lifetime's experience telescoped into an hour or two. They felt dissatisfied, not uplifted, rather fretful, certainly thirsty. The American-cloth bag was lighter now. It was not food they wanted, but a cup of tea.

"Just fits in nicely with the bus. Well, this is a fine day's pleasure for you," said Nanny, walking with assurance into a large and fashionable café where she was stared at.

Sophy sat and fingered her hair-ribbons, watching the people dancing and the pianist's hands reflected in the back-turned lid above the keyboard.

"Leave your ribbons alone," said Nanny.

"That Elizabeth Bennet was beautiful." Sophy took the lump of sugar from its frilled paper case and put it in her cheek.

"Yes. She's good. That's a lovely place she's got up in Beverley Hills, swimming pool and one of those Loggias. Some of the old-fashioned stories make up into a nice film."

"Such lovely dresses," said Sophy. "When I'm eighteen I should like a long dress. It must feel wonderful to walk in." (She sat down, the skirt spread all around her, she laced her fingers in her lap, leaned forward a little and smiled.) "I'd like one like mother had you told me about—the long white one with the tea-rose ribbons."

"Ah, that was a sweet dress. Cream, not white. She wore it to your Uncle Tom's twenty-first. The times I ironed those ribbons and tied them fresh. Everything must be just *à la.*"

Sophy saw herself with everything *à la.* She turned the curve of the stairs, one hand on the banisters, one yellow shoe pointing out of her creamy skirts. Suddenly the music stopped and the dancers in the hall looked up. 'Why, she is her mother over again!' they cried, quite overcome.

"Don't crunch that sugar!" said Nanny.

If you have had a beautiful mother, people expect beauty from you and when they turn away puzzled you feel as if your heart will burst.

"I said don't crunch. Nor suck neither. Another time put it in your cup. A girl of your age and I can't bring you into a café for your manners."

"Did my mother dance?" Sophy, entranced, watched the locked sauntering figures.

"Dance? *She* danced and led all of *us* a dance."

"In what way?"

"Oh, what I was saying over the ribbons, and all the ironing, and losing everything as soon as she so much as laid it down. 'Nanny, I've lost me sapphire ring.' 'There it is,' I'd say, 'staring you in the face as bold as brass.' Plenty of servants in the house then to run about at her beck and call. Not a lot of charwomen." She stirred her tea scornfully. "Yes, helpless as a babe new-born she was."

There was no question of her speaking of the dead with disrespect. She knew well enough ladies ought to be like that; going off for the day in the pouring rain on a horse which was all temperament and vice, fending for herself; or driving the car, coming back covered with oil, talking in the hall about sprockets and such-like, then, later: 'Nanny, do me up! Where's me velvet shoes? Where's me sapphire ring?'

Now Nanny pulled on her mauve cotton gloves and took up the bill. She never left a tip for the waitress. 'What have we had that's been all that trouble?' she asked herself. 'A pot of tea and no civility. They get their wages like anybody else.'

She had taken her standards from lives of idleness and plenty and despised those who worked for their living, and could not pick up a duster now without a feeling of being lowered in her own eyes.

CHAPTER SIX

"Two such idle young men as I have never met," Mrs Veal was saying.

"Yes. You would not easily find our like nowadays," said Tom. " It is money does it."

" What money have *you*? " she asked ; pretending to tease.

" I get my weekly penny from Marion. I am not too proud to take it. I am *so* proud I can take whatsoever is offered and remain myself. "

"Why should he give you *anything*? "

" Because he is sorry for me," Tom said casually.

Mrs Veal did not care for his saying that. She got up, blinking her painted lashes, and pouted.

"Marion was a very busy little man once, when he married, and before," Tom went on. " Even after he came into the money, had the house—still trotting off to his office every morning, kiss wifie's brow, wave good-bye at the gate." He finished the whisky and made a face.

" Why did he pack up, then? "

" He must keep an eye on . . . his house," he said drily.

" Where were you? " she asked.

He gave her a little look and handed her the empty glass. " Oh, I was often here." She took the glass.

It was after closing time and they were shut in among all the sticky, unrinsed tumblers and the cigarette smoke. Gilbert, her husband, had the day off for the races.

She began to plunge the glasses into the tank of slimy, beery water, standing them on end to drain.

" Another one? "

He nodded. Between the tips of his fingers he handed a

pound note. She flushed and shook her head, turning away from him and running a double from the measure.

"Drink it in comfort, might as well," she said, leading the way into the sitting-room at the back. Standing before the mantelpiece mirror, she rolled up her hair freshly, while he sat on the sofa, eyes half-closed, and sipped.

"The little governess," she said. "What is she turning out like?"

He considered. "She is so young, so transparent, life seems to flush through her, to glow from her, like . . ." he looked at the whisky . . . "like wine," he said softly. "And she is honest. It would be useless for her to try to be otherwise. Being so transparent, I mean. And she is brave," he added. "Three things I admire . . . candour and beauty and bravery."

"You said nothing about beauty," she cried, rearranging her fringe.

"That was what I meant when I said about the wine."

She was crisp and annoyed. "Better get some food, I suppose," she said.

"No. Come here."

Holding his whisky carefully, he put out his free hand and drew her down beside him. As she moved she unsettled a great drift of her best perfume, which she kept for Wednesdays—Gilbert's day off.

Tom was quite at home in the room and did not even notice all the things that would have made Marion wince—the china rabbits, the ruched taffeta cushions, the meaningless water-colours, the fringed table runner.

She sat close to him, tapping her fingers on his thigh, a little message which he, for the moment ignored. His surroundings were beginning to dwindle. He slipped his free hand inside her blouse, knowing he must sooner or later, even discovered a paltry, easy pleasure in doing so, but a pleasure incidental to the whisky, until suddenly he felt a

58

violent desire to obliterate himself, to lose himself, to destroy himself and her. She was his hated one, his own lust made flesh, the bad side of his own nature. He vented his hatred on her, he punished her with lust.

But she was a tawdry thing, not worthy of any tenderness. She thought it was pent-up passion he released upon her. . . . She liked the word ' passionate ', using it always in its sexual sense. . . . She would not have understood that he wreaked vengeance on her, used her brutally in his mind.

So close, they were worlds apart.

.　　　.　　　.　　　.　　　.

"Who *do* you love, then?" Mrs Veal dabbed at her eyes, knowing she must not cry, for Tom had said once that it is never moving, always boring and embarrassing for women to cry once they are out of their early thirties. All he had ever said she remembered.

"Oh, Lord!" was all he said now and yawned . . . one, two, three, stretching his arms over his head. Only bad temper *could* have come out of that embrace. "What do you want me to say? Thank you?" he inquired.

If your lover is insulting you must put up with it as best you can, fight your own battle. She could not very well run grizzling to Gilbert to ask him to deal with Tom, complaining of incivility, of coldness.

"One moment you are so . . ." she sobbed, ". . . the next moment so ill-natured and proud."

"I am ill-natured all the time," he tried to explain. 'But I am not proud,' he thought, 'not proud.'

.　　　.　　　.　　　.　　　.

Now it was time to open the bar again, and they had eaten nothing. When he had suggested food, she had begun to cry. If he may not eat, he must drink.

59

"Five to," he said, looking at the clock. It was easy to put her in a good mood; he had only to betray himself, and not even in words, only in their interpretation.

"Come here! Come along!" he said in a different voice. He ran a finger down her forehead, down her nose. "Silly little camel! Stop wittering. Stop being a baby. Smile." She smiled. ('You fool' he thought.) "That's better. Now go and unlock the door. I'll go round to the lavatory and then come marching into the bar the front way, as if I've been at home all afternoon." He smacked her behind quite hard.

"You've had nothing to eat," she said, suddenly apologetic. "I'm so sorry."

"I should damn well think so," he said.

He sauntered out to the lavatory across a little yard with crates of empty bottles and ash-cans. Cinders lay about and pieces of straw. One way and another the stench was awful—'mostly one way,' he thought, kicking open the door. He recrossed the yard, buttoning himself up. 'Kindly adjust your . . .' God, how I hate clichés. How nice to see one day 'Please do up your trousers before opening the door,' or '. . .' He tried out a few phrases, making his way round to the front door.

Two men from the village leant against the bar. He was all right, then, for a drink, his pound note was intact a little longer. They were drinking light ale.

"Whisky for Tom here," said one of them, as Mrs Veal came in from the Public Bar. She and he smiled conventionally at one another, yet there was something reserved, masked about her. He winked. "Good evening," she said quietly. 'What bloody game is this?' he thought. 'Like a coupla kids!' "Cheers!" He sat down on a high stool in the corner and listened to the men talking men's talk. Clichés again. 'They are like two dogs barking at one another,' he thought. 'Sounds come out of their mouths, certainly, but sounds without any significance. " Look, what big chaps we are ! " " That's all they are saying at one another, what dogs say when they bark.'

He indicated their glasses to Mrs Veal and laid the pound note on the bar, unfolded, spread flat, infinitely precious. 'There it goes ! ' he thought. 'There she goes, my beauty.' But better this—better a pound here and there from Marion ('Answer up. Say thank you like a nice boy '), better that than a few more pounds and no time to spend them—rushing round the countryside wrenching babies out of screaming women at all hours, mostly night time, not able to go into a pub in case they say 'His hand was unsteady and no wonder.' 'No, I am quite free,' he thought, looking at Mrs Veal.

"Cheers ! " the men barked at him, lifting their glasses.

"Cheers ! " he growled back and swallowed his whisky. That was good, but it was gone, a mere mouthful. He had forgotten the water. All the same, it had been good, was good, and he leaned back and felt the warmth travelling through him. His change lay heaped up, a pile of silver and coppers. He fidgeted with it, afraid to touch his glass again for a bit. He knew he was drinking too quickly, and on an empty stomach. Then he realised she had given him too much money, that the note had been split up, but not much broken into, and he felt distracted with anger.

Gilbert walked in.

Tom saw her eyes flicker in terror. He knew how shaken she was, how her mind turned over quickly the thought that since he had come early, he might so easily have come earlier, how her world rocked and became unsafe.

" Why, hello, Gil ! " she had said, and now she was saying : "Have you lost all your money, then, or spent it ? "

He shouted " good evening " at them all, slapped his hands

61

down on the bar, roaring for drinks. "Come on, what 'chaving? Don't be shy, boys."

He made his wife run back and forth with glasses. Her face looked drawn and desperate and Tom felt compassion for her, was moved by her at last, but not in a way she would have wished, for his pity would not have fitted into her schemes of romance and fascination. Yet her being pitiable had made her become—for this passing moment—real to him and he wished to be kind and show her sympathy.

He was curt with Gilbert, scarcely acknowledged his whisky. Above all men, this was the one he most hated; the one who represented the great bogus male world (of which he, Tom, was an outcast); who threw money about (Tom drew his heap of silver nearer with a loving gesture); who insulted his wife to prove his grandeur (whereas Tom insulted her because she reminded him of his treachery to himself). Moreover, he had aligned himself with this hated man by taking his wife and letting her make a despicable link between them.

"What sort of day, Gil?" she was asking. "Did Corona run?"

"Did it run!" he exclaimed.

"Yes, that's what she asked!" Tom murmured into his whisky. 'I am having too much drink,' he thought. 'Go steady. Why did he come home so early? He hates me. Nothing to do with *her*, but because I despise what he respects, don't lift a finger to get what he'd grovel for, never laugh at his funny stories about copulation, never slap him on the back or buy him a drink. If I were Marion, he'd call me a cissy and be done with it, but he knows I'm not, that I could thrash the backside off him or any other man and that puzzles him all the more. But he is just right for her, really. He could not have been *made* to suit her better. He is the answer to all she needs and asks for, all that her

62

vulgarity calls forth.' He imagined their love-making; remembered his own; shut his eyes. 'Why does she hanker after me, then?' he wondered. 'Why is she so sick to destroy me? Because she knows I am private and she wants to trespass. She knows I am committed and she wants to annul my commitment. She is worse than he is. She wants to say: " I have received from him the same as *she*—the most beautiful of all women." But who does she want to say it to? She would never dare say it to me, nor to other people—her husband, for instance—and she could never say it to herself, because she knows it is a damned lie. That is why she cries.'

He wouldn't soil his money buying Gilbert a drink, so he slipped it into his pocket and then, without saying good night, as if he were just going out to the lavatory, he sauntered casually from the bar. Once outside, he quickened his pace, going up the warm tunnel of the steep lane, the hedges enclosing him.

There was a lighted window at the lodge. That sluttish woman who was sometimes to be seen slapping a grey, gritty cloth across the kitchen floor at the Manor, stood up in the poky little room, above the dusty leaves of geraniums on the sill, a baby clutching at her untidy hair. She was talking to someone unseen and her mouth moved and her body swayed, as women always sway when they hold babies. 'Do they know unconsciously that they have to keep up the rocking movement of the womb?' he wondered, pausing for a moment beside the gate-post and the broken gryphon. She slapped the baby's hand down from her hair. Above her hung a bird-cage covered with a cloth. All the time, only faintly annoying, like gnats, a wireless bleated. She moved the baby higher upon her shoulder and he could see its bare mauve behind, dinted like an unripe plum.

He walked on up the mossy drive and round the back of the house. There was a light at Marion's window, too, but

no picture, for the curtains were drawn. He knew he would
have to go up and see Marion, because he could not go to
bed with his emotions unresolved, and only Marion could
help him; Marion, and being in that room which once had
been Violet's and where he could never go and sit alone now
without trespassing.

Marion was reading. Marion was polite and never inter-
fered. He asked Tom to have a drink, just as if he didn't
know that he had already had too much, and then, a last
suggestion, pointed to the pot of black coffee on the hearth.

"Wondrous tactful, you are, Marion."

He was so tactful that now he did not make the mistake
of dissembling. He smiled. Tom poured himself some
coffee and drank slowly, his two hands round the cup.

"Why do I do this?" he said aloud. It was a way of
beginning a conversation about himself, which is important
to those who are drunk.

Marion held up his book and read out: "All round it
pipeth chill amidst the orchard boughs; the leaves are quivering and the foliage falls."

"What's that?" asked Tom crossly, baulked.

"Sappho."

Tom always called Greek a dead language. "Never
thought of it being Autumn there," he said, "or leaves
falling. Or orchards."

Presently, Marion read: "O Hesperus that bringest back
all things which the shining dawn dispersed, thou bringest
the sheep, thou bringest the goat, thou bringest the boy back
to his mother."

"And the drunkard home from the pub. I told you many
times it's a dead language."

He put an elbow on the mantelpiece and Marion glanced
up a bit anxiously at his thousand-flower dishes. When he
bent his head again to read, Tom looked down at the streaky

gold hair, the black velvet jacket he despised, the long fingers in a fan over the back of the book, and felt the knot of his emotions draw up tight.

" Marion, you remember the time you told me to come down off the stables' roof and I wouldn't? "

He looked up and smiled.

" You broke your arm," he said. " I expect I said ' I told you so '."

" No. You were very quiet and gentle. As they were lifting me, I kept fainting and coming back and each time as I fell into darkness, I knew you were there, being steady, and waiting to help me."

Marion fingered his book, a little embarrassed. He knew Tom was going to say: " It is the same now." He did so. Marion waited, looking at the printed page as if for assistance. He realised that Tom was drunk, but he did realise, too—which is rare in people who drink for pleasure, not obliteration—that Tom wanted to use his drunkenness as a screen behind which he could strip himself of thoughts, emotions, which burdened him.

" I am drinking myself to death," said Tom. It was melodramatic; but, like all melodrama, had the seeds of great tragedy in it. " I am wasted. No use. I am done for."

Marion closed his book. " In a different way, I am done for, too." he said.

The clock ticked, the fire shuddered and a little brittle noise came from the hot side of the coffee-pot, for the coffee was beginning to boil and Marion moved it back, away from the heat. Tom stared at him, leaning there against the mantel-piece, his elbow among the china bowls.

" I am *reading* myself to death, that is all the difference is," Marion went on, rapping a knuckle against the cover of the book.

" Why? "

65

Marion said nothing. Then Tom asked: "Money, you mean?" and he nodded.

'This money, this house, ruined us both,' Tom thought, looking round the room, and then at his cousin. 'It gave you Violet. That was the root of the trouble.'

'It is useless to blame the money,' Marion was thinking. 'If I had to go to that office every day, I should be the same man. I should come back eventually to my books and my painted bowls.' "Margaret makes up for us both," he said aloud. "Look at her energy and her worthiness and her public spirit—all the Committees and the petitions and the campaigns."

"And now a baby," said Tom, looking away. (Violet screaming, he thought. She screamed like an animal, not a human sound. She had frozen the world with terror. She had been beautiful in early pregnancy, had moved him so deeply, reminded him of mediæval sculpture, the drapery falling, the pleats widening over her belly and her bosom so heavy, so utterly different. Later, she had become swollen, her face, her hands puffed out . . . But he had promised her not to remember. . . .) He covered his eyes with his hand and one of the bowls fell into the hearth. Now it was a thousand pieces.

"It doesn't matter," said Marion.

'I have even broken his bowl,' Tom thought stupidly. "I think I shall go to bed," he said.

"Don't go like that," said Marion. "Don't go, feeling sorry for yourself."

"You know everything, Marion. How is that?"

"I only know things out of books."

"I think I *shall* go to bed."

"All right."

Tom looked for a second at the smashed china in the hearth. Marion put him at peace with himself. 'If he knew

66

about Mrs V. even, he would never be disgusted,' he thought. ' He would only read something to me out of a book.' " All things which the something dawn has what? " he began.

" Dispersed," said Marion.

" I'm sorry about that bowl."

Marion said nothing. He had said once that it did not matter and he had spoken the truth.

" Good night."

When Tom had gone, Marion knelt on the rug and picked up the pieces of china. He filled another bowl with the coloured fragments and then sat down again and opened his book. The ormolu clock gave out eleven notes and each struck a little chime, a little jarring reverberation from one of the thousand-flower bowls upon the mantelpiece.

CHAPTER SEVEN

"SOME QUEER THINGS are going on in this house," Nanny said to Mrs Adams from the lodge. "Things we've never been used to. There was Mrs Vanbrugh the other day complaining about the glucose going, then I find me *Picturegoer* in the larder lying there as cool as a cucumber on the shelf. It was the day we saw *Pride and Prejudice* and I left that paper on me rocking-chair. That makes me think, so I take a look around—cream cheese missing, and the bread sawed about anyhow. It's this so-call governess. Don't she get enough to eat or what?"

"She don't look no more like a governess than I do," said Mrs Adams, blowing her sandy hair up from her face as she scrubbed.

"Into the corners!" Nanny suddenly rapped out.

"Thursday's me day for this floor. I'm only giving it a do-over."

"Too many do-overs in this house. Nothing done right. Thursday you'll get one of your funny turns, I daresay. Then where will the floor be?"

'Where it is now,' Mrs Adams thought. She fanned out the soapy water over the flagstones, then gathered it up on the slimy cloth, wrung it into the bucket and shuffled backwards on her knees.

'She's no good for gentlemen's service,' Nanny thought, watching her. "A good do-out of a room, I like," she said aloud. "Into the corners and behind the pictures. Then you know it's all sweetness, nothing skimped."

"You could spend your life on your knees," Mrs Adams said, thinking of the great house. "We all like our little bit

68

of shut-eye after dinner. And our look at the paper. Half the world scrubbing on their knees, the other half sitting on its arse. That's what it looks like to me."

"They've got their own ways of being busy. Up here," said Nanny, tapping her forehead. "Where'd we be if it wasn't for the head-workers?"

"That's what I'm saying."

Mrs Adams shuffled out backwards through the door to do the last bit, the bucket pulled scrooping after her.

"That's a lick and a promise if there ever was," Nanny said, watching her. "Slopping dirty water over it; it'll be worse than before. Once it's dried. You'll see. Them flags always look nice and fresh wet. Wait till they're dry, that's all." After a while, she went on: "When it comes to me doing her job for her, then I begin to see the dawn. Just at the last moment having to cut extra sandwiches and then running for the bus like that takes off all the gilt. Either that or miss the Forthcoming Attractions and the News as well, more than likely." To herself, she thought: 'Them Grecian lessons! Do they think I was born yesterday?' But she would not imply criticism of her employer to a mere charwoman, a daily woman, paid by the hour, who left, she now observed, the half-wrung-out cloth in a slimy, smelly twist in the bucket.

Mrs Adams came rocking back across the wet floor on her heel-edges, not to mark the clean flags. "That job's jobbed," she said. As she put up her hand to straighten her hair, the inside of her arm showed grey and crêpy. "What now?" she asked, wanting to get back to her baby.

But Nanny had feelings only for the babies of the well-to-do, and even then, it was the baby's belongings which inspired her most, the tools of her craft—the piles of dazzling folded napkins, the curved blue safety-pins, the padded baskets, the enamelled kidney-bowls. Then she was all-powerful, surrounded by such accoutrements, sitting on the low chair, the bath-apron over her lap, the napkin folded ready, pins in her mouth. . . . " Is he a diddums? " . . . one hand clasping the fat ankles together, the other fondly smacking the creased buttocks, then flouring the wrinkled, mauve, hanging genitals with powder . . . "and is he a diddums?" . . . the little feet fighting in her hand. Oh, all that was long since. Mrs Adams's baby was not a proper baby, was female, did not smell sweetly, was not real and could not matter, so: "There's the stairs yet," she said. "If anyone should so much as run a finger down them banisters, I don't know, I'm sure."

Mrs Adams was tired and worried in her heart, for all her tart answers; and the baby, though female, though such a trouble with wind, was real to her and tugged her homewards. "Just a flick round then," she conceded, and went off with her duster to wipe down the banisters and rub up the more horizontal surfaces of the furniture.

Nanny feigned eccentricity as Hamlet feigned part of his madness, and for more or less the same reason, so that she could speak her mind, set herself apart from humanity and tell the truth, keep her integrity in words, at least, and have every allowance made.

"Oh!" said Margaret, coming so silently and quickly into the kitchen. "No cinema then, this afternoon?"

"They kept the big film on all the week."

"And was it a nice film?" Margaret condescended, in order to gain time, find her reason for being there.

"It was Russian," Nanny said flatly, not caring for foreign countries unless the English aristocracy was settled there. "What are you up to?"

Margaret came and stood on the red and black rug.

"What is it now?" The old woman could hardly stave off the sleep stealing heavily over her.

70

Margaret said: "It's Marion. I wanted a cup of tea for him to take with his tablets."

"One of them heads again. You'll have to make it yourself, then. The kettle's warm. Funny he gets these turns. A drop of warm oil down his ear, I'd try." ('One of her darlings, Violet's youngest brother, turning his fist against the side of his head, crying. "Lay your head on Nan's lap. Nanny's got you!" 'Never liked to hear one of the boys crying. Violet was always crying anyhow. Not the boys. When he fell asleep after his warm milk, it was lovely seeing his cheek against the pillow so peaceful. . . .')

Margaret went to the larder, put milk and sugar on a tray and cut herself a slice of custard tart. When she had made the tea and tiptoed back through the kitchen, Nanny was asleep, her shiny, crinkled hands lying like toads in her black lap.

Marion was walking up and down his room.

"What's this?" he asked, suddenly checked, seeing the tray.

"Tea and some tablets."

"How did you know?"

"I thought at lunch . . ."

He was surprised by her sudden goodness. "And what is that?" he went on, bewildered by the slice of tart lying beside his cup. 'Did she think he was going to eat it?'

"Oh, that is for me," she said calmly and took it up and bit off a corner. "I hate nutmeg," she said, eating lovingly. "Nanny wants you to have warm oil in your ear," she went on, laughing to herself; but she could really only think about the eating, turning the tart this way and that in her hand thoughtfully; baiting Marion was too stale a sport. It belonged to her childhood, and Tom's. In those days Tom had turned on him impulsively, savagely, because he could not bear that one emotion—pity forcing him to feel uneasy.

71

It made him impatient, brutal, curdled his kindness. Marion, with his gentleness, his cleverness, his girlish ways was such fair game at school, among other boys. Since Tom had not the character to stand beside his cousin and defend him, he had made a loud noise to confound his better nature and led the bullying himself and, with strange, mixed impulses, swung from day to day between indifference and the devising of new cruelties.

Margaret's teasing had been feline, less spasmodic, longer sustained, reflecting herself and her love for her brother, and had never really ceased.

Yet Marion (the thin fair boy, tied by his bluish wrists to the beam in the garage, not crying, although knowing he would not be set free until he did), that Marion, grown-up, had won in the end, for the adults' world was different from the children's: in the children's world he had encountered every brutality of flesh and spirit; in the world of grown-ups he had won the house and Violet (she bracketed them in her mind, the house set above the woman).

"One of your bowls is missing," she said, to make conversation. "Who broke it?"

"Tom. It was an accident." He had finished the tea and he wished she would go.

"Well, I didn't suppose he threw it on the floor on purpose. Was he drunk?"

"He was a little—blurred. I don't know about drunk. But the bowl was nothing to do with that . . . it was an accident." The pain down the side of his head had the shape of a flower. It grew on a fine stem from his jaw, put out tendrils across his cheek, leaved and budded, and there, below the eye, the pain's centre, it burst hotly into bloom.

"Why do you tolerate him?"

"Tolerate whom?" He was preoccupied with pain and could not follow her conversation as well.

72

" 'Tom.'"

" I do not tolerate him. I love him."

" Surely men don't talk of loving one another."

Her look of fastidiousness amused him.

" A man with neuralgia may talk of anything."

She thought : ' It would be a pretty sort of eternal triangle with homosexuality thrown in as well.' Aloud she said : " But the money you give him."

" Now you are getting a little out of your depth," he suggested. " A little confused."

" Tablets working yet ? "

" No."

" Why do you give him money ? If he had none, he'd have to do some work."

Marion thought : ' I took his work away from him all those years ago, when I took away the motive of his work, the meaning of his life.'

" Why don't you answer me ? "

" Because I am hoping you will go away and leave me in peace."

" No, Marion. You have plenty of peace. Your life is so full of it, you might be an old man or an invalid. But I'm not discussing your life, only Tom's. Stop giving him money, make him go away. There is this awful woman in the village. Please put an end to it." She had finished her custard tart and there was nothing left to do with the long afternoon but make a scene.

" What awful woman in the village ? " He despaired of being left to deal with his aching head in privacy, and sat down at the table, a hand across his cheekbone.

" There you are ! You live in your ivory tower . . ."

" Oh, must we have all that clap-trap ? Say what you will, but spare me your clichés."

She did not look offended.

73

"There is a very horrible sort of woman at the pub. Tom stays there after closing time. She's the wife of the publican."

"I know nothing about the village," he said with indifference.

"No. I always hated and despised the old Squires and their Lady Bountifuls with their meddling and condescension and their giving back in charity a mere hundredth part of what they had pillaged. But you are worse. You keep the hundredth part, take no responsibility, show no interest, give nothing to the land even, but let the soil go sour and the grass rank. The people who once lived in this house would not have seen the land lying useless, or one of the villagers starve or go without coal at Christmas, and if a girl was in trouble by a man, they'd damn well make him marry her. . . ."

"I don't feel cut out for that," he said laconically.

"I never thought I'd be upholding the feudal system," she said with amusement, taking a walk to the window and back, wondering what her friends in London would have said. "Tablets not worked yet?"

He moved his head slightly to say no.

"Odd!"

He wondered if she were so cruelly obtuse with her patients, decided not, could even imagine her sympathetic and helpful, with working-class mothers, for instance, those she approved.

Now, she said, polishing her engagement ring, looking at it from the length of her arm, as if it were something new:

"Well, I wish you would speak to Tom."

"Speak to Tom! He is a person, not a child. Even if he were a child, I am not his nurse."

"Then don't behave like one."

"I should go down to the village and plead with the woman for your brother's honour, if I were you."

She went out in a temper, closing the door not at all quietly. The sound splintered across his face.

．　　　．　　　．　　　．　　　．

After supper, Marion asked his aunt: " Have you a good recipe for soup for the poor?"

Margaret laughed. " There is a good one in Mrs Beeton . . . Benevolent soup it is called."

" The name appeals to me," said Tom.

" It is mostly turnips and lentils, I believe."

" Did you say *Bene*volent?" Tom inquired.

" Lentils make a good enough soup." Tinty looked fussed. " But if it is only for a joke," she said, " there is the recipe your great-aunt wrote down. I seem to remember looking at it one day in the library." She went out and returned with a green silk-covered book filled with pale handwriting. " Here it is! The Beef Tea for the Villagers."

" Oh, heavens!" cried Tom, for the villagers were his friends and enemies and could not be unified, even with beef-tea.

" But this would never have done," said Tinty. " Three pounds of beef. . . . draw to the side and beat in eggs. . . . Brandy, two wine-glasses . . ." She peered at the page closely . . . " Yes, that's right. . . . brandy. My goodness!"

" Mrs Beeton is less generous," said Margaret.

" It is a pity letting soup get into the brandy like that," said Tom.

" My duty seems to lie before me more clearly," said Marion, looking at Margaret.

Tinty fluttered the pages of the little book, not understanding. Cassandra sat quietly by the window, knowing that she had at last seen in Marion the ruthless indifference she had feared in him from the first, and though the conversation had fogged her, she could only wonder why Margaret

75

did not die of shame instead of taking up her knitting so calmly.

"All this talk about soup," said Tom, jerking himself to his feet, "although it is beyond me, has given me a thirst."

His mother sighed, but only after he had shut the door. Margaret looked across at Marion as if she waited.

"Cassandra, will you walk round the park with me?" he asked suddenly, avoiding his cousin's glance. He had not used her Christian name before, and Margaret's astonishment was palpable, humiliating to Cassandra herself, who said nothing, only murmured and ran to fetch a jacket from her room.

CHAPTER EIGHT

SOPHY watched them go, lifting her bedroom curtain a little to one side, saw the sun outlining their hair as they crossed the park, growing smaller, walking with bowed heads beneath the elms. Then she turned from the window and looked at herself in a mirror; the white cambric nightgown fell like a bell from her shoulders, her hair was tied up in its night ribbons. She unknotted them, combed out the plaits with impatient fingers and shook her hair back loosely, feeling it fan the small of her back; then she smiled into the mirror, eyes sidelong, fingers laced provocatively across her mouth, like her mother's in the photograph on the dressing-table. But she was born without colour and biting her lips, pinching her cheeks, brought only a fleeting glow. She drew the thin stuff of the nightgown taut across her chest. Sometimes, looking down the length of her body, lying in bed, she fancied she could see the shape of her breasts beginning, but it could only be her ribs curving away shallowly on either side and now, through the nightgown, the bones showed in rows, nothing more.

She took a piece of cucumber from the mantelpiece and rubbed it over her forehead to remove or discourage her freckles. 'If I didn't do it, I'd have more,' she comforted herself, squeezing a little juice on to a mole. Perhaps in the morning she would awake divinely pink and white.

When she had finished, she threw the cucumber out of the window on to the weedy gravel below and watched a lop-sided brown hen rush, tottering, at it, stab it with its beak half-heartedly and retire with it into the rose-garden. Then she climbed into bed and took up her diary. She wrote:

77

"Pliny about Vesuvius this morning. When my father came in, Miss D's hand trembled. He says I shall not begin Greek for the present, he is too busy teaching her! ! ? ! ! Fancy having to teach a governess. Anyone who reads bad things about themselves in this book have been spying and therefore deserves it. Margaret finished knitting some little shoes blue with forget-me-nots. I pray I shall never have a baby. Of course, not everybody dies or else they wouldn't take the risk. Tom goes out more and more. He never stays at home and when he does it isn't worth it. He goes to the inn and has sherry and his fingers are quite brown with smoking. He is far more handsome than my father being darker. He says I am a morebid little fool going to the churchyard. But I didn't think he was polite when he picked a yellow rose off my mother's grave and put it in his button-hole. It was too much like stealing from the dead to make yourself smart. I said when my father dies a red rose would grow on his grave and twine with the yellow ones like Lord Lovell. It was then he mentioned about being morebid. But why was he there himself if it is so morebid, keeping company with the dead, he said. When we were coming back across the park he asked me wouldn't I like to go to board-ing school. He is always asking me wouldn't I like to go and why don't I ask my father. I said I would drown myself if they made me and he sighed heavily. But it will stop him saying any more about it if he knows my life is at stake. It makes me quite sick even speaking about it so I know I should die because I should cry every night if I had to go.

"Now they have gone across the park, my father and Miss D. What are they saying about me? I hope they decide nothing horrible. Nanny found three eggs in the rose-garden but when she broke them into the basin the smell was awful. It is that brown hen hiding them I think, the one which just eat the cucumber."

Then she turned the page and dipping her pen into a different coloured ink, wrote:
"*Marks for the Day*."
Without hesitation, she summed up her day's behaviour.

" Goodness.   Fair.
Helpfulness to others. . . .   Held M's wool for her, fed hens,
ran errand (Liver salts) for Aunt T.
Industry.   Made bed.   Learnt vocab.
Did the Pliny.   Forgot to turn the mattress, though.
Bravery.   Not.
Honesty.   O.K.
Prayers.   A good ten minutes.
N.B.   Must not be morebid any more."

The mauve ink filled her nails. It had been a good deal
of writing for a little girl and had all to be gone through
again the next evening. Her life seemed burdened with her
own rules. She put away her writing things and lay back
(one pillow only lest she should grow a double chin). There
was still the anti-dream formula to be gone through. " Please
God defend me from all nightmares, dreams about China-
men, or gibbets and tumbrils or coffins, or cellars and caves,
or snakes and any reptiles or unpleasant creatures, or
burglars, or ghosts or skeletons and do not let me be chased
or shut up or frightened and do not let me see Thee in a
vision because I am not worthy. And last of all, dear God,
in your great goodness, do not let me dream anything at all."

She lay still, looking at the darkening ceiling. " Or
vampire-bats," she added, and fell asleep.

.   .   .   .   .

They had crossed the park, as Sophy had noted, and now
they came to rank grass and the broken boundary fence lying
in the nettles. Beyond a·little stream the ground rose more
steeply towards woods. Marion led the way along the fence,
and crossed over a little bridge. They walked through sorrel
and clover and came at last to a summer-house, built as a
Gothic ruin. It was carefully contrived to look like a fragment
of an old abbey and yet not let in the rain.

" There is a little water-colour of this in my bedroom,"

said Cassandra, sitting down on a stone seat over which he had spread a large yellow silk handkerchief.

"And I have a pen-and-ink sketch of it in mine," he said. " I think all the young ladies of the house used to come out here with camp-stools and governesses and sketch-books."

"Perhaps I should bring Sophy."

"My dear, I didn't lump *you* in with the camp-stools."

She was by now so much in love with him that she was ready at all times to take offence at what he said.

"The woods are most Radcliffean," he went on. They were indeed darkly green and menacing and emitted a flustered bird from time to time, a jay with a horrid squawk, or a wood-pigeon breaking out of the branches as if it fled from demons. Before them the plaited water went idly past, weeds of great brilliancy wavering above the mosaic of white and black and yellow stones. There was a smell of fungus and rotting leaves and water.

"What happened about Sophy's little cat?"

"It died. And was buried."

"Why do you suppose she kept that from me?"

"It was when I first came. I don't know. I asked her to tell you. . . ."

"And she wouldn't? After all, I gave her the cat."

"Perhaps that was why."

"No. Who else knew? Tom?"

She was flurried, wanting to lie to him, but unable, because she was nervous of committing herself either way.

"Yes."

When it was necessary to ease her silence: "You must think this a very odd household."

The sun set, leaving the tops of the sorrel ruddy and luminous, the grass lay this way and that, full of shadows, every blade separate. The mist moving away across the distant prospect of the park was in keeping with the Gothic woods and ruin, and Cassandra, sitting there with the broken flint walls arching above her, felt that she was unreal, an engraved figure in the end-piece to an eighteenth-century romance—and Marion as well.

" I believe you tried to spare me something," he said. " But there was no need, you know. Parents should not have to be protected from their children. What do you think about Sophy? I should like to know."

She looked away from the park, the cadenced levels wreathed in mist, and laid her hand flat upon the yellow handkerchief between them, looked at it as if it would give her some inkling of how to express what she felt.

" I think she ought to go away from here. To school," she said, thinking of her father, of Mrs Turner, and then of Sophy.

He took up her hand and let it lie in his own, but his touch was impersonal and light, as if she herself stopped short at her wrist. If it had been a strange flower or shell lying there curved and shallow he could not have looked at it with less reference to emotion. In his searching way, he learnt and analysed. It was the way he had examined her face, she remembered, the first time she had seen him standing by the window in his room in that sudden unfamiliar flood of sunshine.

" If she were to go, you would go too."

Her finger-tips crept a little inwards towards her palm and tightened, so that the nails left the imprint of four half-moons in the hollow. Then the fingers uncurled and relaxed. He sensed that she was agitated and he put his thumb over her palm and smoothed out the little dents.

" Apart from Sophy, do you want to go away? "

In her agitation her heart cried: ' I love you.' Aloud in a prim voice, she said: " No. You asked me about Sophy. And that was what I told you."

The scene somehow missed being quite so idyllic as it would have looked as the tail-piece of an old-fashioned love-story.

"What would you do if you left here?"

"I hardly know."

He gave her back her hand as if it were something he had borrowed, that he was punctilious about returning. For the first and only time she imagined what it might have been like to have been Violet, and pitied her; saw with clarity, for what it was, the titillation of Greek lessons, the cerebral intimacy, the impersonal taking up and dropping of hands. When one is young the blood bounds forward at a finger's touch, something is—not intolerably—suggested, for the touch is an adventure in itself and may be hoarded, taken to bed as a child takes a present, turned over and contemplated and treasured. It is something complete to be kept a lifetime and, moved in a million different lights, remains always the same, unimpaired.

With mutual assent they began to walk homewards across the park, the sorrel and the coarse, bleached barley-grass whipping at their ankles. As they came near the house they saw that the bluish-green wooden door to the wall-garden was open. It swung back and Tom came out with a woman. She stood by, waiting, while he closed the door, and then they walked away round behind the empty stables, very close together and his hand brushing her thigh as she moved. Her head was bent. She was eating red-currants out of her hand.

Cassandra blushed. As they passed the wall-garden, a scented warmth seemed to steal out of the bricks. They exhaled a heavy sensuousness, a suggestion of stored ripeness, like the ambient mellowness of a woman very conscious of her power to distract.

Marion said nothing. His face was quite a blank.

When Cassandra reached her own room, she stood for a while by the window, turning her hand, the hand, one way and another in the near darkness. Then she curved it so that it was like a scallop-shell and ran a thumb thoughtfully across its palm.

CHAPTER NINE

How OBTUSE the sensible may be, Cassandra discovered after lunch the next day.

She was not to be Miss Dashwood any more, it seemed, except to Sophy and Aunt Tinty, for Margaret, opening her bedroom door a little, called across the landing to her, using her Christian name. Sophy was lying on her bed for half an hour, reading an old bound copy of *Little Folks*. When she had rested they would go for a walk, collecting grasses in the park, to be brought back, classified, and pressed between pieces of clean blotting-paper.

Margaret was standing before her long mirror in a petticoat, her frizzy hair untidy from trying on frocks.

"Oh, Cassandra!"—like anyone putting aside the formality of a surname, she used the alternative unnaturally often—it seemed to have a tiresome attraction for her— "Cassandra, I was just wondering . . . would you care to have this frock? I shall never get into it again. It clips in under my behind and will burst asunder soon across the chest. With a little pleat here and here and a bit of easing in on the shoulder, it would be all right. It is scarcely worn."

But the frock was Margaret and could not be otherwise.

"What do you think? Try it on."

Meekly, but outraged, Cassandra slipped her shoulders out of her blouse, let her skirt fall to the floor. Margaret dropped the frock over her head and began pulling in and tweaking, pinning, going round the hem on her hands and knees, pins fringing her mouth. Cassandra, from her superior level, studied the room, the opened drawers revealing a rich untidiness of clothes, the mannish dressing-gown with all the grandeur of looped and whorled and twisted cord, the large shoes lying about.

"Now look in the mirror." Margaret sat back on her heels, her belly rounded beneath the white slip, and her face flushed from all the crawling and bending.

Out of the wide sleeves Cassandra's arms emerged pathetically, mauve against the cruel blue of the dress.

"There, that looks heavenly on you. Much better than on me," said Margaret enthusiastically. "Will you let me cobble it up for you, then?"

Expressing gratitude did not come easily; what would come even less easily would be the miserable business of wearing the dress, as obviously she would now have to.

"Ben always liked this dress," Margaret went on with simple pleasure. Everything she said to enhance the gift, detracted from it.

Cassandra left her sitting on the window-seat, her bare arms among the folds of saxe-blue, the silver thimble tapping and flashing, her face calm with goodwill and satisfaction.

The landing smelt of warm carpet; the kitchen cat lay in the patch of sun which spread in the shape of the window across the floor. Cassandra tidied her hair, picked up her wild-flower book, put on the look of a governess and then paused to listen, fancying she heard running footsteps along the passage.

.   .   .   .   .

Sophy stood in the doorway of Tom's room. Her face was so pale that it reflected her red dress. He was sitting by the window drawing.

"Have you run away?" he enquired.

"It was time for me to get up, but she just didn't come."

"She?" His pen scratched and finicked on the paper.

"Miss Dashwood?"

"Oh, yes."

" What are you doing? "

" What should you think I am doing? "

" Drawring," she suggested.

" ' Drawing.' Don't talk like a baby."

She came nearer and looked over his shoulder.

" What is it? It's like a skeleton with a bush on his head."

" The arteries of the body."

The fine leaves wavered out like the fingers of a sea-plant.

"Or one of those natives dressed up like a tree. A medicine-man. What's it for? "

" Are all your drawings *for* something? "

" Yes."

" Oh, I see."

" How do you remember how it all goes? Is it what you have to know to be a doctor? Does Margaret know all this? " She watched with half-closed eyes, the hair-fine sepia lines fascinating her.

" It is all immensely inaccurate and rather old-fashioned, the bastard of art and science."

" Miss Dashwood says the word differently."

" Oh, she does, does she? "

" She says ' bastard '. Like that."

" And does she use the word frequently? "

" It comes in *King John*. It means an armour-bearer."

" Is that how Miss Dashwood explains it? "

" No, I just somehow guessed it meant that."

He did not remain grave, as the well-intentioned child-lover would have done. He burst into laughter.

" What *does* it mean then? " she asked haughtily.

" A bastard is a . . . a hybrid."

" A hybrid? "

Cassandra could be heard calling.

Sophy went to the door. " I have to go and pick a lot of bloody grasses," she said.

"Harsh language is not delightful in a woman," he said. It was not altogether true; for her mother had often used the coarsest expressions, but with such coolness and finesse that the shock gave a little tap to the blood, as if she had rapped one flirtatiously with a closed fan; yes, it had been the equivalent of that Edwardian gesture.

"Sophy!"

"Well, run along, run along!" He turned irritably to his drawing.

She opened the door and peeped out. "I'm coming," she called. "*Au revoir!*" she said to Tom over her shoulder.

He winced.

"Did you say 'hybrid'?" she popped back to inquire.

He nodded.

"I don't know what that means either."

"Run along and pick your grasses, for God's sake."

When she had gone, his pen dropped to the carpet and stuck there, quivering by the nib. He could not bother to pick it up, but leant back in his chair and closed his eyes.

. . . . .

Tinty, as a young mother, had dammed up the flow of her children's emotions. Indifference is a hard state to maintain, but they had done so, faced, they thought, with a worse alternative. By checking their own tears, their own anxieties, they hoped to check hers. In a small way they had succeeded, but it was nothing compared with the vigilant care which had gone into the effort. Their attitude of heartlessness and immunity had served them well at school and would have served them well indefinitely except for the fact that life cannot always be nudged aside nor love answered and quietened by casual bantering. They had never had practice in dealing with urgent emotions and in such a crisis they could draw on no more experience than an infant. Such a crisis had not arisen for Margaret. Tom had been early overthrown, had failed to recover, and now cloaked himself in melodrama—the laconic drunkard or the sordid roué—to put himself beyond the reach of his mother or other women, or men.

As a child, like Sophy, he had kept a diary. Coming from school one day and finding his mother lying down with a soaked handkerchief pressed to her eyes, he knew she had been prying. She pried still. His drawings could only puzzle her. He no longer wrote a diary. He received no letters. (He remembered, as a boy, the patient, gentle and expectant voice at breakfast: " Who is your letter from, dear ? " and his fingers folding the paper, slipping it back into its envelope —" From a friend, mother," and Margaret giggling.) The skeleton of his life was not fleshed over with the clutter of friends and their messages and confidences. Yet still he felt the presence of his mother in his room when he returned to it at night or after lunch. His drawings looked, he fancied, as if they had been scrutinised, his closed desk seemed to warn him mutely, everything looked touched, altered, bearing an imprint. To-day, two of his tablets were missing. He pondered this, lolling in the chair, watching the pen quivering in the carpet like an arrow.

.   .   .   .   .

Tinty was going to take the tablets and lie down. She was flustered and frightened about it, the first time she had taken such a drug. She was convinced that her low spirits were linked with her low blood-pressure . . . (Margaret with a scornful smile, strapping her arm round and pumping up some peculiar gadget . . . " There you are . . . perfectly normal . . . what did I tell you ? . . . Oh, mother, mind that, do ! It cost the earth . . ." " All the same . . ." she had begun, but Margaret had snapped up the wooden case and turned away) . . . the little tablets, she knew, would accelerate her pace and lift her spirits. A friend she had once made in a boarding-house had fallen quite a victim to them and had described her sensations delightfully, how she rose to fantastic levels of happiness so that she was too gay to go to sleep at night and was obliged to take more tablets to put herself to rights.

Tinty, depressed about her son at the time, as at all times, had begged to experiment; but the friend was firm in her resolution not to set another on the primrose path. Tinty had never forgotten that glimpse of the forbidden. ('I lie down feeling like death and quarter of an hour later spring up and wonder what the hell I was lying there for,' and 'When it wears off? Why, then I take another.')

Now, still troubled about Tom, she had stolen his tablets and, scarcely wondering how or why he came by them, had shut herself stealthily in her room, wound up the clock and set it right, drawn the curtains, and now, taking the tablets with a sip or two of water, swallowed them both. She lay back, her brittle grey hair spread over the pillow, and closed her eyes, relaxed and quiescent, like a good patient going under an anæsthetic.

.   .   .   .   .

They had collected rye-grass and waybent, quaking-grass and cock's-foot, vernal-grass and crested dog's-tail, foxtail and purple moor-grass.

Down by the lake, yellow frogs leaped away from them and Cassandra stifled the repulsion which she felt, and went bravely towards the bulrushes with which the lake was nearly solid. The sight was a little fantastic, they stood high, closely serried, the rusty plush heads very still, but the reeds sometimes clashing or lisping together, hanging so sharply bent over, so folded, like a child's drawing of reeds.

Sophy cut her hands pulling one out. It was taller than Cassandra and she carried it tilted like a lance. "We can't press this in blotting-paper."

Cassandra agreed, trying to find a little firm ground, free of frogs, to walk on.

Sophy had laid down her grasses to pick the bulrushes and now they were lost.

" It doesn't signify," she said.

"Of course," Cassandra felt bound to say, "they are really not bulrushes at all, but reed-mace. Bulrushes are quite different."

" I shall go on calling them bulrushes," said Sophy.

Cassandra had once said exactly the same to her father. He had replied : "There is nothing more beautiful about a thing than what is true." She had not believed him then and did not now and sympathised with Sophy, thinking : ' Beauty is not all it is cracked up to be, or Truth. There are curious, moving, exciting and fantastic things as well.' She wished she could have explained this to her father; now it was too late. The dead cannot be answered back, the last word is always theirs.

Sophy's thoughts may also have been with the dead, for she said : " Let us go back through the churchyard and down the avenue."

Cassandra, unlike Tom, thought it useless to check her morbidity. At the edge of the churchyard, by a little rubbish heap, some pink thumb-bruised poppies with grey leaves had seeded themselves. Sophy laid down the bulrush and began to gather a bunch of poppies. "My mother's favourite flower," she extemporised. Cassandra stood about among the heaps of dead leaves, waiting.

" I shall go and sit in the porch," she said at last.

But Tom was sitting in the porch already. He received her as if she were paying him a call or as if they had an assignation. It seemed quite the usual thing. They sat together on the wooden bench among the missionary notices, behind them the cool darkness of the church and before them the sun on the gravel and Sophy running among the yews with her bunch of pink poppies.

" She should not be encouraged," Tom said, folding his arms across his chest, closing his eyes, as if preparing for a little nap.

" In what? " Cassandra asked, although she knew.

" These prowlings round the churchyard."

" Isn't it wrong to wrench people away from the dead? "

" No, it is right. Especially with young children. Yes, *wrench* them away. That is the word."

" To stifle grief makes it worse."

" I doubt if that is true. Besides, what grief has she? "

" Missing her mother."

" My dear Cassandra! " He opened his eyes and laughed, then closed them again quickly. " She was born as her mother died. Their souls had barely time to salute one another in passing."

" All the same," Cassandra went on stubbornly, " she misses her. One can miss what one has never had."

" That sounds like Marion. I should like to get Sophy away from here. There is altogether too much of death about the place—the very house is mouldy." He moved restlessly. Then handed her a cigarette out of a crushed packet. " I am glad she has you, because you are young, but I wish you would not encourage her in this about her mother. Fantasy can be damaging. Reality can't hold a candle to it, everyday life doesn't stand a chance. What is she doing with all those poppies? "

" Putting them on her mother's grave, I imagine."

" She talks to you about her mother often? "

" Yes."

91

" What sort of things? "

" Repeats what she had dragged out of Nanny, embroiders it, I am sure, spends her energy inventing what no one will tell her. She feels she lives in the shadow of her mother's beauty, I do know that. Someone should tell her what she wants to know. If her father can't make himself do it, *you* should, or your mother. People are very selfish about death, increase the suffering so needlessly, so unnaturally." She had finished thinking about Sophy and was thinking of herself. " They will never let you talk about the dead. It embarrasses them. It is only *their* convention—that you must not discuss your mourning, to save them taking trouble. It is to keep *their* minds off sorrow, not the bereaved. . . . They know that isn't possible. One only wants to talk . . ."

" Is it your father, or your mother? " he asked, under- standing, resigning himself.

Her mother had been a comfortable woman, necessary to her as a child, warm, brave, seldom put out, but unable to provide for ever what her daughter needed, and Cassandra had turned to her father's learning, seeking someone who threw longer shadows than herself, as the young do.

So—" My father," she now said to Tom.

" Tell *me* then."

" Oh, I miss him," she began. " He taught me so much. He loved books and walking in the country and knew all the names of the flowers and how they got them, and about architecture and old churches. We used to go bicycling and doing brass-rubbings in the holidays." (Tom yawned.) " He was much older than my mother and, I think, lonely. In the evenings he used to sit in his little room and prepare lessons and correct exam-papers—he was a schoolmaster—and he always had a glass of weak whisky to sip as he worked. . . ."

" What do you mean by weak whisky? "

" With a lot of warm water in it. And he would read

amusing things to me that the boys had written. He rarely spoke or seemed to think about himself. The evening he died, he said: 'You'll have rain to-morrow.' He was looking out at the sky and it was the last thing he said. He seemed not to mind about to-morrow, although he knew he would not be there. It would still exist, because of us. He was never angry, never anything but gentle . . ."

'What a boring old man,' Tom thought. He had asked for it, though.

"In books, death is just a sad chapter, and then you turn the page and go on with the next. But really it can't be left behind quite like that. It goes on and on, a sort of nagging parenthesis, coming in brackets at the end of everything that happens . . ." She fancied she saw her life spread out in handwriting on a page and again and again in the recurring brackets ' My father having died.'

'A parenthesis?' thought Tom. Death had not been that to him. It was his life which went into brackets.

"What about your Greek lessons? Do you still have them?"

She looked glad and yet confused when she nodded.

'What does she want, a tutor or a young man?' he wondered, not remembering what it was like to be twenty nor that the answer was 'both'.

"Was her mother *so* beautiful?" she asked desperately.

"Oh, Lord, yes."

"The photograph in Sophy's room . . ."

"Oh, *that*! One day I will show you my drawings of her."

Coolness and the odour of worm-eaten wood came from the church. She got up and went to the door and, putting her handkerchief over her head, went inside quietly. He smiled at her, especially at the bit about the handkerchief, then settled back and seemed to doze.

93

Light fell from windows of plain greenish glass beyond the pillars, but the altar was chequered with ruby and indigo and sepia from the bad modern glass of the East window. She tiptoed over stones and gratings. Madonna lilies in a stage beyond full splendour, stood in brass vases and shed pollen on the cream and yellow embroidery. It was a curious silence in there, as if the outstretched effigies were keeping quiet, but only for a little while.

When she got back to the porch the gravel blazed before her on the other side of the shadows and she stepped suddenly into the full warmth and perfume of the afternoon, the desultory murmur of pigeons and then the sound of footsteps on the path.

Tom sat up with a start, plucking a little yellow rose from his button-hole and letting it fall down behind the seat.

"Ah, there you are!" said Sophy. "I thought I heard voices a little while ago."

"What were you doing?" Tom asked.

"I was putting some poppies on my mother's grave."

"She never liked poppies," said Tom, yawning.

Sophy's mouth stiffened. She turned and walked away down the path in front of them. Tom looked neither to left nor right. At the side of the path was Violet's grave with its rose bush and the jar of poppies, wilting already, their heads leaning down as if sick.

"I feel like a cup of tea," said Tom, the traces of his mid-day whisky in his mouth still. "I *will* show you the drawings one day. Yes, I should like to." Then he added: "When I *do* tell her something about her mother it is wrong, apparently." For Sophy walked on ahead, seeming offended.

As they climbed the lyre-shaped steps before the house, Margaret saw them and leaned from her bedroom window, calling, and holding up the blue frock in great triumph.

.   .   .   .   .

Little worries about food disturbed Tinty as she lay on her bed in the darkened room. If the sausages were 'off' as she half-suspected, what then could they have for supper? It had to be something easy, for it was Nanny's cinema day and Mrs Adams had the baby ill with croup.

And all the time as the clock ticked on, her disappointment grew. She felt no inclination to spring up, crying: 'What the hell am I lying here for?' The tablets were taking a long time to raise her spirits. 'Serve the sausages with an onion sauce,' she thought. 'And warn Margaret beforehand. Then I had better go down and prepare the sauce at once.' But she lay a little longer and presently fell asleep.

Margaret woke her, shouting to the others from her window. Tinty swung violently out of her sleep, lay whimpering a little like a small dog; she had dribbled from the corner of her mouth. When she saw that it was nearly half-past four she slid off the bed and cast white powder over her face until it looked mauve and bleak. She rattled back the curtains, straightened the bed. 'Nothing happened,' she thought. 'Nothing different.' She had a dull headache from sleeping in the daytime, otherwise nothing. Full of little worries, she hastened downstairs to get the tea.

CHAPTER TEN

"An old pal of mine—Mr Smart."

"Pleased to meet you. That's no recommendation, though," said Gilbert, shaking hands across the bar.

"Heard a lot about you, of course. Worst pub in these parts, Charlie said."

"Good old pal—Charlie," said Gilbert, with a gesture of cutting his own throat. "What're we having?"

"Double brandy, since you so kindly ask," said Charlie.

"Half of mild for Charles," Gilbert called over his shoulder to his wife.

Tom sat on his corner stool drinking his fourth whisky. On summer evenings he hated this cool, beery interior and the same old backchat across the bar, and Mrs Veal, moving nervily under his scrutiny, pathetically blasé, flirtatious with a little group of car salesmen, travellers and bookies, her every gesture calculated to inflame him, whereas nothing moved him any more but whisky, and all her hard work was wasted, unless it could be that she was satisfied in some way merely imagining the hidden fires consuming him.

He drank in the pub and suffered the irritation of it, to postpone that last stage of being alone with the whisky, a stage wherein the hours would lose their significance, for there would be no closing time, no reason for stopping. He felt lately that he could for only a very little while put off that final phase, knowing that he was losing grip of the whisky, that it could not be taken any longer in a desultory way, that he must be alone with it and in darkness, to concentrate all his senses upon his struggle with it, in order to wrest from it some paroxysm of delight.

A dreadful metaphor had occurred to him—that his conflict with alcohol was sexual and he like a starved and frantic woman striving by intense yet hopeless concentration to find peace from a casual and heedless lover. Always the culmination was beyond reach. 'A deeper drink,' he thought, 'something to strike deeper so that all the congested longing might be discharged, the blood flow back through its accustomed channels promising peace for a long while.' He drew his new drink to him and closed his eyes. The neat whisky slipped over his tongue into his throat; but, as always, it evaded him. It faintly warmed, flirted a little with him, withdrew, mocked at him. It was a hateful metaphor, he thought.

A shout of male laughter startled him and his hand shook. Mrs Veal had turned away coyly from their conversation, stood sipping her Guinness, eyelids cast down. If she did not actually blush, she gave the impression of just having done so.

'Oh, God, they posture before me like madmen,' Tom thought, feeling like the Duchess of Malfi—that they with their disease and lunacy were put there to destroy or torture him.

One of them, one of the madmen, with a curt gesture to Mrs Veal, included Tom in his round of drinks. The whisky was bought for him in contempt, a coin tossed from a pile of winnings towards some mumbling old whore, he thought, drinking it because neither the whisky nor he himself could be damaged by the other's insolence. Mrs Veal placed it before him and stayed nearby. He would not look at her. When he had finished this drink there would only be one more and then home, for the coins in his pocket had dwindled: like a blind man, he had learnt to know them by fingering and turning them; he would not bring them out to look at them.

He damned the woman for standing so close to him. She

ruined his act of concentration. He knew she deplored this rapid drinking, but hoped to salvage some brutality from it for herself at the end. In a few minutes he pushed the glass towards her again.

.　　　.　　　.　　　.　　　.

Marion read Sappho to Cassandra. The words seemed to have been brought up, glittering, dripping, from the sea, encrusted still by something crystalline, the fragments and phrases like broken but unscattered necklaces, the chipped-off pieces of coral, of porphyry, of chrysolyte.

Cassandra half-listened as she wrote out her declensions, trying to evade the pain and impatience in her heart and that picture, always before her during these lessons, of the little girl, Violet, reading Homer at the age of eight.

Marion stopped reading and sat watching her, her intent face and her smooth hair dropping against her cheek. He felt his relationship with her to be of the deepest intimacy, and his gift to her the most precious he could bestow. He sat still, the book drooping in his hand, and watched her pen shaping the unfamiliar and beautiful letters.

After they were married, Violet would never read with him and they never again came near to the intimacy of their betrothal, for she never opened a book nor took up a pen. Instead, there were always people coming and going or she would disappear for long days on her own; then came her uncontrollable gusts of crying, her sickness and restlessness, and his deep pity for her keeping them apart since it forbade his disturbing her or adding to her distress. She had died without turning to him again, and he remained where he had always been, alone in his room—Marion *contra mundum*, as Tom used to say at school— and more than ever set apart by those months of delight before he had married Violet and changed and indirectly killed her. He had been

98

so oppressed by this idea of his guilt towards her, of blame, that he had spoken of it to Tom, the only occasion when he had asked his help, and Tom had seemed irritated by his sentimentality and said coldly: "One scarcely intends murder when one loves a woman. It is what is called a remote contingency," and he had walked away repeating and savouring his cliché to himself. He had always warned off those who approached him for sympathy, and Ruskin's advice 'Never be cruel, never be useless' he deliberately turned upside down and was never kind except to those who were in no need of his kindness and never useful to anyone for a single moment.

Cassandra lifted her eyebrows as she wrote—although it was more like drawing than writing—and the skin went tight over her forehead with her effort of concentration. She was transparent because slowly-matured, he thought, wise from books only, and with the innocence of a child.

'Oh, God, make him touch my hand again,' she prayed, copying out βασιλεύς from Violet's old primer.

"Cassandra!"

She looked at him quickly.

"Don't be imposed upon. Your good manners lead you into mistakes. You know what I mean. That dress. Don't be made to wear it out of kindness. It is so much Margaret. Not you."

She said nothing.

"I think you're depressed. Let's fetch ourselves a bottle of wine." He pushed his chair back and got up, much pleased with his idea. "I have to be very mean and secret about my wine," he explained, taking up a bunch of keys from the mantelpiece. "Come down to the cellar with me."

She wrote βασιλεῦσι and laid down her pen.

The house seemed to absorb people after meals. In the drawing-room Tinty sang a sentimental ballad: somewhere

99

between the notes of the untuned piano and her warbling flat old voice the melody itself lay untouched—"The End of a Perfect Day." On the top of the piano there was always a pile of music she had bought as a girl—the piles of music (mended with gummed transparent paper) which all girls had in those days when Tinty was young and wore bronze shoes and large black bows at the nape of her neck and hid the scented leaves of Papier Poudre in her Dorothy bag. 'Cynthia Fowler' was scrawled across the music covers with their ornate scrolled titles—"Where My Caravan Has Rested," "Absent," "Nirvana," "I Hear You Calling Me," and the pictures of nouveau-art lilies, of bulrushes, had been filled in with pale water-colours on far-off wet evenings, long ago at the turn of the century.

The cellar door opened out from the old bakery, the medieval part of the house, upon which the Palladian façade had been imposed. The bakery was full now of old mangles, swede-mincers, vinegar casks, knife-grinders and heaps of broken flower-pots. A little mouse ran round and round inside a sack of maize. The kitchen cat had left a torn-up chaffinch upon the floor. It was all eaten away except the frail, outstretched legs and feet, fine-drawn and exquisite, a feather or two and some lead-coloured entrails.

Margaret crossed the flagged passage from the kitchen, eating a slice of bread-and-dripping on which they could see the dark jelly and the sprinkled salt. Cassandra's mouth watered, although, on account of her love-sickness, the worm i' the bud, she would have refused food in Marion's presence.

"How *can* you, Margaret?" he asked, sorting out his keys before the locked door.

"For whose benefit is the cellar locked?" she enquired. "Would you care for some beef-dripping, Cassandra? My cousin does not keep what I call a good table."

"You must speak to your mother, then," said Marion.

"No, thank you," Cassandra said coldly.

"No one *eats* in this house," Margaret complained. "I no longer have erotic dreams, because they are all about food now—great squidgy gingerbreads full of almonds and lardy-cakes, warm and greasy, and ribs of beef and treacle-pudding . . ."

"Good God!" said Marion. He opened the door and the chilly, fusty smell came up from the cellar.

"No, I wouldn't touch your wine, my temptations are all with things to eat," Margaret went on, leaning ungracefully against the wall. "As far as I'm concerned, never lock the door. And Tom, as you know, doesn't drink wine."

"The door is locked because of the stairs," Marion said haughtily. Cassandra had observed that his cousin did not bring out the best in him, he became stiff and touchy. "Sophy might break her neck if the door were left open."

But Margaret had gone back for more bread-and-dripping.

"What do you think you would like?" Marion asked, and his voice echoed down the steps before him.

Wine had not been much drunk in Cassandra's home, although there had been the Sunday ritual of her mother's lunch-time sherry. While she was dishing up, Cassandra's father would carefully fill a small ruby-stemmed glass and she would have it on the draining-board and sip as she made gravy or strained greens, then she would bring the glass to the table and drink it while her husband carved the joint. Sometimes Cassandra was given a half-filled glass, and sherry would always, she thought, have that association of roast meat and the smell of Yorkshire pudding and the sound of her father clashing the carving knife against the steel.

"Sherry—do you think?" she asked uncertainly.

Going among the bins, brushing aside cobwebs, he was happier than he had been for years; he felt another personality approaching the frozen silence of his own, something he had not expected since his last failure of all, his failure with Sophy. When they came up again and opened the door, Margaret was still mooning about the kitchen.

"Would you like a glass of sherry?" Marion was forced to ask.

"I don't drink sherry. There's a cobweb on your sleeve. When you've drunk all that"—she waved her hand at the cellar door—"it's gone. You draw on the old stuff, but you lay nothing down. Like everything else you do. You just hope it will last you out—this house, your bit of money, your mode of life, your wine."

Cassandra looked awkwardly away.

"I have enough money," said Marion, locking the door. "I think I have enough wine."

"Ah, Tio Pepe!" cried Margaret in a different voice, seeing the bottle under his arm. He led Cassandra away as quickly as he could.

"The Little Grey Home in the West," Tinty quavered in the drawing-room. Plonkety-plonk went the old piano, which had the damp in it, and sounded as if it should be on a concert-party platform.

"How unbearably depressing!" said Margaret, following them into the hall, but she left them at the foot of the stairs and went in to her mother, and the singing and the piano-playing stopped at once and querulous voices arose in their stead.

.   .   .   .   .

The men had reached the stage of confidences, the deepest confidences of all, business confidences. Now their voices were serious and there were no further bursts of laughter. They were putting one another on to good things. Mrs Veal was banished to Tom's end of the bar, for this was even more big boys' talk than the stories about sex which preceded it. Charlie knew all the dodges and they listened to him with respect; he had woven his way unnoticed in and out of the fringes of big business and now interlaced his talk with famous names.

"Yes, I picked up a lot of useful knowledge there," he concluded, and finished his light ale.

"It has only been useful for boasting," Tom said in a low voice.

"Shush!" Mrs Veal implored. As she swept a damp cloth over the bar, she picked up his whisky, wiped underneath, and murmured softly, leaning forward: "If you go out, wait by the pergola and I'll be out in a minute."

They were not busy, but Gilbert would be unable to leave the bar. Tom said nothing, but he drank his whisky quickly and got up and went out, so that she became fretful with impatience, wanting to follow him at once, but holding herself back for a little, for appearance's, not her dignity's sake.

Tom walked straight out of the pub and up the road.

.   .   .   .   .

There was nothing of roast beef in this sherry, Cassandra thought. It had no Sunday morning associations for her. It was essentially a drink for the violet hour, the cool summer airs, the earth reeling over into darkness and flowers stiffening their petals against the night; it was quiet in the mouth, like olives.

"You chose better than might have been supposed," Marion observed.

"But you know I hadn't imagined it being like this," she said in a sudden unloosening. Her eyes added: 'Ask me what you please and I shall tell you.' Her head was like a globe of shifting flakes; when she moved, it became full of confusion like the snowstorm in a glass paper-weight.

She rested her shoulders against the green watered silk of

103

the chair behind her, sitting on the rug with her thin pinkish glass like a convolvulus in her fingers.

"Your profile is like my mother's cameo-brooch," said Marion. "A lovely straightness about you—very rare, that." He pulled open a little drawer in the table beside him and took out a brooch framed in finely-beaten gold. Then he could see that the cameo profile was quite unlike hers in reality, having a Greek nose and the mature sloping line from chin to neck the Athenians—and Edwardian English—appear to have admired. He supposed that any clear-cut profile against a darker background has the same intaglio quality.

She put her glass on the table with great care and stood rocking a little on the hearthrug.

"Dear Cassandra, you are a little drunk, I think." He took her chin in his hand, and ran his thumb over her eyelid and the bones round her eyes. She felt at peace with his fingers touching her face and the wine shedding its radiance through bone and blood and tissue.

"Have you ever been drunk before?"

She moved her head slightly. He laughed and put an end to his connoisseurish perusal of her. She picked up the brooch and looked at it in a puzzled way.

"What's this owl for?"

"The lady is supposed to be Night."

"And what are these?"

"Poppies."

"And this is the moon, I see."

"'The stars about the fair moon . . .'" he began and, continuing in Greek, he took the brooch and pinned it to Margaret's blue dress.

"Why do you do that?"

"Because I mean you to have it."

"I could never wear it," she said quietly.

"If you can wear that dress to please Margaret, you can

wear this to please me," he said, deliberately misunderstanding.

"But the reasons are different—don't you see?" The snow had begun to sift and slant in her head and she closed her eyes for a moment.

"No, I don't see. Yes, I do, really. But I still mean you to have it. I think you ought to go to bed now. It's after ten. I'm sorry if I gave you more sherry than you wanted."

"How tactful you are!" she said sleepily. She went lingeringly across the room, looked out of the window for a moment, paused at the door and said: "Thank you for my Greek lesson," laughed and disappeared. Marion went back to his chair and filled his glass.

Going along the dark passage she thought: 'He wanted to get rid of me.' Then she fingered her brooch and put up her hand and stroked her eyelids, ran a thumb round her eye-socket.

"What *are* you doing?" Tom asked, coming upstairs. "Why are you wearing Margaret's dress? What are you doing wandering about in the dark?"

"I've been for my Greek lesson."

"Come here!" He stopped by the landing window and looked at her. "You're—not quite yourself?" he suggested. "Greek lesson is a good name for it. Your eyes don't focus."

She could well believe it, but feigned alarm.

"In fact, you're drunk, my dear." Her mouth drooped.

"Where did you get that brooch from?" he asked suddenly and in a different voice. With a foolish gesture she laid her hand over it.

"Who gave it to you?"

He grasped her cold elbows and began to shake her gently. "Tell me where you . . ."

"Marion!" she cried. "He gave it to me." Tears began to flow down her cheeks.

"How dare he!" Tom whispered.

Margaret's door opened and she came out across the landing, her dark hair on her shoulders, the long nightgown held in the medieval way bunched up in her hand over her swollen stomach.

"Tom, my dear, what is going on? Cassandra, why are you crying?"

"You look quite beautiful, Margaret," her brother said in a surprised voice.

She could not take a compliment gracefully and became surly at once. "I suppose you are drunk, Tom."

"No. I am enormously sober. Cassandra, do you want to go to bed?"

She nodded.

"Don't let Margaret keep you up, then," he said politely.

When Cassandra had gone, he turned away, too.

"Where are you going now?" Margaret asked.

"I am going to say good night to Marion."

All the way along the passage he was whispering to himself—"How dare you, Marion! How dare you!" But when he reached the door of Marion's room he checked his anger, as if he were suddenly conscious of danger lying all about him.

"So you are sober, Marion?"

"Of course."

"Cassandra is not. She was wandering along the corridor looking like Ophelia and wearing Violet's brooch."

"Where is she now?"

"I sent her to bed—out of Margaret's way."

"Where was Margaret then?"

"Oh, you know what Margaret is. She has a row with Mother and goes to bed at nine out of pique, feels refreshed by ten and ready to interfere with other people's goings-on."

"What goings-on were there?"

"I was man-handling Cassandra. I was about to take advantage of her by the landing window."

After a second or two, Marion asked: "So you thought you would get in with your story first?"

Tom considered this carefully and then said "Yes."

"I dare say you have made it sound worse than it was!"

"Yes. I only had her by the arms—the cold part of the arms, above the elbow. After her Greek lesson I had no hope of rousing her."

"Don't talk like Nanny."

"*Why* was she wearing Violet's cameo?" he asked.

"I gave it to her. It was my mother's. I can't remember Violet wearing it often."

"But she *always* wore it, with those print blouses, the lilac one and the grey striped one—and with the black velvet . . ." He turned and walked to the window, having forgotten himself. ('The situation is fraught with danger,' he thought.) He looked down at the bleached steps before the house. For a while after Violet's marriage the façade had blossomed with lights; on evenings like this, women in pale frocks had been led down the steps among the colourless moths which encircled the lamp, they had gone looking for romance, sitting under the cedar trees on white seats, had returned to the house later, their faces reflecting neither rapture nor disappointment. He and Violet had not looked for romance, but had walked in the darkness, fingers locked tightly together. One night, he had thought of Rossetti's picture "How They Met Themselves" and felt that at each turn of the shrubbery they would see Tom and Violet coming towards them, the white and indigo of their clothes in the moonlight, the pale, laced fingers and the darkness of their eyes. But no vision had molested them, nor underlined their guilt. There never had been any ghosts and were none now; neither in this room, nor across that lawn where the monkey-puzzle tree stood so black and barbed against the fainter sky.

Had he borne with every sort of torment, watched Violet marrying Marion, seen them driving away to their honeymoon (very cool and remote, she had waved her gloved hand), so many times said good night to them on the landing, and sat with Marion the afternoon she died, conceding to him the greater grief, now to be broken by a trivial business of another girl wearing her brooch?

" Mother's having quite an evening," he said, making an effort. For even up here in Marion's room, they could hear the faded songs and their unsure, but rubato, accompaniment. He turned his back on the window. " Do you really teach Cassandra Greek?"

Marion put his forefinger in his book and looked up. " She has reached the fourth declension."

" She is so insipid," Tom complained. " She clasps her hands like a governess in a book. She ought to wear long skirts."

" *All* women ought to wear long skirts."

" I couldn't agree more. Especially out of doors—the long drapery flowing back from the thigh—the Winged Victory, for instance."

" Hardly governessy."

" No. Bombasine's the stuff for *them*, I believe. I think I'll go to bed. If you're in love with her, Marion, I'm sorry I said she was insipid."

" I'm not in love with her."

" Well, good night."

" Good night." Marion began to tidy the room. He picked up Violet's Greek primer and Cassandra's exercise book and put them together on his desk.

.   .   .   .   .

" What happened to your besotted boy friend?" Gilbert asked, getting into bed.

CHAPTER ELEVEN

CASSANDRA STOOD in the old bake-house arranging the flowers. The only ones to be found were the hardiest perennials; even so, she hoped to achieve something arresting. She carried her great flower-piece of sunflowers and magenta phlox into the kitchen and, leaving them on the table, went back for the honeysuckle.

" I always thought them colours clashed," said Mrs Adams, who was rubbing up some of the silver and drinking tea.

"And so they do," said Nanny. " Makes my eyes wince to look at them."

" Did she have a cup? " Mrs Adams nodded towards the bake-house.

But governesses are not quite servants in the usual sense of the word: their education puts them out of reach of the continual flow of tea which goes on in kitchens.

" She did the bowl of fruit nice," Mrs Adams went on.

" That's a pretty apple, that wine-sap; but I'll lay the vine leaves are done for before evening. Just like all these young girls. I remember Miss Violet over the cold collation—' Let's have it all green and coral, Nan,' she used to say, and there it'd be—great lobsters lolling here there and everywhere on beds of lettuce, cucumbers sticking out in all directions, sliced down lengthwise and cut out like crocodiles with prawns for tongues, everything smothered over with green mayonnaise and red pepper. It *looked* lavish enough, but who could eat cucumbers like that; it was mostly left, wasted. A stand-up buffy, too, and the lobster not rightly cracked, and Mr Tom fixing a claw in the hinge of the library-door and pulling it to—till I rapped his knuckles for him, passing by. All the young gentlemen out on the terrace stamping on lobster with their boots. And laugh! 'What goings-on!' I said to Miss Violet afterwards. She knew I didn't like it, but they didn't care, being half-cut at the time. I was just saying," she added slyly, as Cassandra came back into the kitchen, " you remind me of young Mrs Vanbrugh with your flower-arranging. She always liked something a bit different. I remember——" she turned to Mrs Adams again, "—one day she came in and said : ' Such an idea for the table to-night. I wonder I've never seen it before.' She gets out the flat bowl we used to have tulip heads floating in when that was the rage and fills it with moss and toadstools—all different kinds, puff-balls and red and white spotted ones and those wavy ones like bits of shammy leather. ' It smells a bit earthy,' I made so bold as to say, but young ladies and gentlemen are tough, nothing puts them off their food. ' How lovely! How original!' I expect they said." (Her voice rose in imitation of the gentry.) "I can well imagine. Well, in the morning, she was laying-in till lunch, of course, I went into the dining-room first. There it was—quite collapsed—'eaving, a writhing mass of maggots. When I told her she laughed. ' You can't better the mauve sweet peas in the silver table-centre,' I said. ' All that with grass and mirrors and wild-flowers—shells full of convolvulus, that was another one—it doesn't really do. I like smilax on a table, myself.' "

" That's right," said Mrs Adams, nodding.

Cassandra was held. She stood by the table, fingering the marigolds.

" Oh, she always saw a picture in her mind and it had to be like that. ' I want it all to shine softly,' she says—' branches of honesty and candlelight and me in me pearls and me ivory chiffon.' So, upside-down the house is turned till she gets her way. Or, no! it shall be dark ivy trailing out of that very fluted vase you have the sunflowers in. Then I knew she was up to her tricks—that Grecian frock *he* designed for her and real ivy leaves in her hair—not artificials—and long trailing bits. She went and pulled them off a grave in the church-yard. And sandals with her toes out; mind, she had no corns: it was all right as far as that went. 'What's she up to to-night?' Cook used to ask. All this for some dry old professor or what-not. Well, it was for herself, really. She didn't care if the others thought her queer as long as *she* was satisfied. Nothing spoilt her looks. How many of us can say the same?" Nanny rocked in her chair, her cup and saucer held high. Sometimes she sipped, tilting back, her old, beetleish appearance, lined, yellowed, seemed wistful, but was not in reality. Cassandra, with her palely-coloured young face, intent on the evocation of beauty from the past, looked wistful, too. And was.

Nanny had disapproved of Violet, but disapproved of Cassandra even more. She had always loved her boys and was not above setting the girls against one another; whether they were dead or alive. It delighted her to bring Cassandra to the edge of despair about Violet.

Margaret came into the kitchen, with the purposeful and deliberate tread of a pregnant woman, as if battling her way through obstacles.

"A nice cup of tea, madam?" Mrs Adams asked, to cover up her own sipping, really, but she made her words sound like a Salute to Motherhood with the deference in them.

Margaret had a feeling away from tea. "One of those things . . ." she began, drumming her long white fingers on the deal table, which was so scrubbed that the grain stood up in ribs. "Metabolism," she murmured to herself. The word was so Greek, so clear and sharp and so unlike the Anglo-Saxon language of the old wives. She did not care for female-talk, as she called it, unless it was very far removed

III

from women gossiping over gates or over the four o'clock fire; unless it was clear, decisive, scientific.

"I remember with Miss Violet's mother, that was with the youngest boy," Nanny began—('Oh, God! She's off!' Margaret thought. 'I might have known.')—"Heartburn! I've never known anyone to suffer so. As soon as she so much as sat down to the table. 'You mark my words, madam,' I said, 'that lad'll have a mane of hair'—I knew it was a boy, she carried so high—and when he was born, there it was, like black feathers down to his shoulders."

"How revolting!" said Margaret. "What was that to do with the heartburn, though? And a boy is carried no higher than a girl. How could it be? And why?"

"A *doctor* should know," said Nanny, putting down her cup. "A nice drop of tea, Miss?" she asked Cassandra at long last.

"Thank you." She felt under a spell, standing there in the kitchen with the other women, the day outside beginning to get hot, the smell inside of honeysuckle and plate polish.

Still rocking softly, Nanny took the pot from the hob and poured a tan-coloured stream of long-brewed tea into the steep white cup. "I've never known it fail," she was saying. "With Madam she carried the boys right under the bust, it was much remarked upon, but Miss Violet she carried so low that she could never as much as go up the stairs without sitting down half-way for a rest, that's when we began having the chair on the half-landing. Then trouble with her water. 'I've been in and out of bed all night, Nanny,' she used to say. Pressing on the bladder, you see."

"Just how it was with me," said Mrs Adams, but knew at once that she had gone too far, putting her own pregnancy alongside those of the upper middle-classes. "How about when Miss Sophy was born?" she asked, to make amends and hoping she was in for a treat.

"Oh, that!" said Nanny. "Too many tears for us to see *what* was going on there."

"Kidney trouble," Mrs Adams whispered at the coffee-spoons, laying them in a row, bowls cupped together.

"Eclampsia," said Margaret—another Greek word. "Do you *eat* anything with these endless cups of tea?" She looked restlessly round the kitchen. But 'endless' annoyed Nanny and she said nothing.

"Do you feel like anything to eat, Cassandra?" Margaret asked, putting her into a desperate position. She could not make up her mind which camp to move over to. Luckily, Tinty came into the kitchen at that moment to discuss lunch and make a few rock cakes.

"Two hospital nurses Miss Violet had at the end, full of long words the both of them," said Nanny darkly. "For all that, she had fit after fit. They couldn't stop it. I shall never forget the sight of her, her hands as stiff as frozen fish and the thumbs lying across the palms. Her face was purple."

"For goodness' sake!" cried Tinty, making wild little gestures behind Margaret's back. "I'm ashamed of you, Nanny." Desperation for her daughter's peace of mind made her brave.

Margaret laughed. "I've seen it before," she said. Nanny decided to take it out on Mrs Adams, hoisting herself out of the rocking-chair, feigning great age; she pounced on the silver rose-bowl, just finished, standing on the strip of green baize, reflecting the dresser with its blue cups and Mrs Adams's elongated face.

"Look at this!" cried Nanny. "Is it done, or what? Smudge here, tarnish there, thumb-prints all over. I've always taken a pride in me polishing—rub till it's white as a diamond."

'Misplaced sexual energy,' Margaret thought, slipping into the larder. She hated polishing, herself.

Tinty spread the bluish raisins on the table.

" Are these all we have? "

Margaret was rapidly making them less.

" That's all," said Nanny, off-handedly. She was not a cook, nor a housekeeper. She only stayed because they were all frightened of her and might as well pay her wages as any other of the families she had bullied in the last forty years. It was as convenient a home as she could expect, unless next door to a cinema, which would mean a ' bad address '. Her life had woven itself into this house, since the day when Miss Violet's mother (the only woman she had ever feared) had sent her to look after Miss Violet in early pregnancy. She had known it would be the last job in the long sequence of nursery life. A good life. With authority and ritual. There had been interesting confinements, plenty of male children, involved and interesting feuds with governesses, midwives, housekeepers and fathers, even death. Now she sat in the rocking-chair, shelling late peas, and with a suggestion about her that her frail old body was being taxed beyond its strength.

" I'll make out a list," said Tinty. " Is there anything else we need? I'm going in this afternoon."

" I'll take you in the car," said Margaret. " I can see if there's any double-satin ribbon."

Tinty began to look desperate. " I can see for you, dear."

" But you'd have to go on the bus."

" I enjoy going on the bus."

" Rennet," said Nanny. " And vinegar."

" Nut-meat roll," wrote Tinty. " Irish Moss. Catarrh-herbs."

" Well, six yards of cream double-satin ribbon," said Margaret. " And my calcium tablets. If you insist on going alone. It will give me a chance of writing to Ben."

Mrs Adams scraped carrots now, humbly silent.

"I must go up to Sophy," said Cassandra, picking up a bowl of marigolds.

"You'll get worms eating those raw carrots," said Nanny to Margaret.

．　　　．　　　．　　　．　　　．　　　．

"*Patter heemone ho en toiss ouranoiss* . . ." Sophy droned inking in the grains of the schoolroom table. Marion sighed. He was walking about the room, jingling some keys or coins in his pocket, very depressed, very impatient.

"Stop, Sophy!"

She had stopped anyhow and looked up mildly.

". You are ink up to the elbows."

She looked at her finger-nails and then reproachfully at him, her glance suggesting that he had exaggerated.

"You hate this?"

She nodded.

"Your mother could read Homer at the age of eight. What do you say to that?"

"It was very young," she suggested politely.

"She knew it was the key into the treasure-house, you see. Why are you yawning so much? Were you late to bed?"

"No." She had been writing her journal, though, long after the light began to fade.

He picked up an exercise-book from the table and glanced through it. "Never let your hand-writing slope backwards, Sophy." He read for a little and then aloud: 'So poor ill-fated Mary looked up yet once again into the tumultous vacuity of the star-canopied empyrean and the muffled oars beat sonorously upon the turgid surface of the lake.' What is this?"

"History," said Sophy.

"Who wrote it?"

"I did."

"I don't know about 'history'. It might be Amanda

Ros going for a row at night. What did Miss Dashwood say?"

"She said I had a tortured way of expressing myself."

"And all these words . . . I suppose you cannot resist them. Perhaps you will be a writer." 'What would Violet have done with this shadowy child?' he wondered. 'Would the disappointment of not having handed on her own beauty have been bitter and rancorous?'

"Go on learning your Lord's Prayer till Miss Dashwood comes back," he said abruptly, and went out of the room.

"*Patter heemone . . .*" Sophy began, but she soon stopped. Perhaps, then, she would be a writer, since she was so plain to look at. She tiptoed across to the mantelpiece mirror, held back her hair from her temples, sucked in her cheeks until she looked interesting as she believed, and desperately ill and like the picture of Baudelaire's mistress. It would not do to be too healthy. She looked with tear-filled eyes into the glass.

"Sophy, dear, what are you doing?" asked Cassandra, as she came in with a bowl of marigolds. "Have you finished your lesson, then? Are you unwell?"

"I had a feeling of lassitude."

Cassandra sat down and opened some books.

"Perhaps a little parsing will dispel it," she said in the schoolmistressy voice with which she often dismayed herself nowadays. She was sometimes alarmed at the idea of this voice gaining on her in the years to come, until she had no other, until it was the scar her profession had left upon her, as sure as a tatto-mark, as distinguishing.

•   •   •   •   •

Tinty suffered increasingly from the disease which had killed her mother, the disease of anxiety, with all its haunting persistency, its continual seeking for new forms in which to manifest itself. Her late husband, who had died (more robustly) on some battlefield, had said in their early married life—"Tinty is half the time anxious that she may be pregnant, and the other half worried insane because she is sure she is barren."

"Is the child quite normal?" she had insisted, after the easiest of deliveries. "Are you perfectly sure he is not bowlegged? And then his eyes wander so oddly." But the child was normal and the milk 'came down beautifully' as the nurse said. All the same, nothing stopped Tinty. She weighed, she filled in charts, she pored over books and then over napkins. She snivelled in bed over every nursery upset, every chafed behind, every teething-rash. The children's lives seemed to depend on so tenuous a thread. She went to their funerals a hundred times and more. Fussing can be a delicious pleasure to some; but anxiety is killing. It ate away all her vitality, for one test of endurance followed another—Margaret had gland trouble, Tom had pneumonia, they both had whooping cough: household pets were ill, were lost, were run over, died: servants caused crises and ' unpleasantness': Tom had to go to boarding-school and would surely be homesick, bullied, underfed. He would die suddenly of appendicitis or rugby football and she would arrive too late for his last whisper, after an exhausting train journey, more familiar to her by far than any actual travelling she had ever done.

But her husband's death she bore with fortitude and equanimity. It was suddenly an accomplished fact and had not been much dwelt on beforehand, because at the time, Margaret was in quarantine for chicken-pox and having her liberty-bodice undone every hour for inspection. Into the words and phrases like 'incubation period', 'contact', 'isolation', 'temperature', and so on, the stark words of 'missing, believed killed' seemed quite unreal and not to be assimilated.

As the children grew up, Tinty was left alone with her own

daily ailments. One winter morning she had coughed up a little blood. Margaret was helping her to make beds at the time. Poor Tinty sat on a chair and tried to wonder what she would do at the Sanatorium, how it would alarm and depress her to see the other patients growing weaker, dying. "That's only blood from the upper air passages," said Margaret, seeing the handkerchief, the stricken look.

Tinty lived through a month of agony, waiting to be X-rayed; sat, at last, like a pauper on a bench waiting her turn. Her lungs—she heard much later, when she was quite worn-out—were unimpaired.

The next week she coughed another red streak. "Perhaps they were wrong," she suggested. Margaret walked out, slamming the door. She did not understand that her mother really did suffer and only wanted to be at rest, and could not be.

This afternoon Tinty felt that she had escaped. 'And now,' she thought, sitting in the bus which rattled its way through the flat, unremarkable landscape, 'if only,' this new doctor she had found in the town and to whom she went so secretly that he might have been known to carry on some more disreputable profession, 'if only he would say, with a fine, straight look—none of Margaret's evasiveness— "There is no cause for anxiety. No cause whatsoever. Your heart . . ." ' But at the very thought of the word she began to fringe her bus-ticket, blink back the tears, for a tap was turned on in her head, it seemed, letting down a great, obliterating stream of anxiety.

The men who climbed into the bus at the "Blacksmith's Arms" brought with them a prodigious smell of beer. As the bus had turned round at its terminus, they had come noisily out of the front porch, the barmaid (Tinty supposed) waving a hand and then slamming the door.

. . . . .

" Time *if* you please ! " said Mrs Veal.

" The lady don't make us very welcome."

" Whell oi guess it's toim oi whas off."

" One for the ditch."

" *Time*, I said."

" I've a kind of feeling we're not wanted. . . ."

" Whell oi guess oim . . ."

" Now *come* along," said one of Gilbert's friends, taking a firm line. " Lady's licence to be considered. Finish up, lads."

Gilbert was at Stockton for a few days and The Boys were rising to a kind of gallantry towards his wife, collecting glasses, calling time. Drunkenness they would deal with for her, but there was none. Like Sixth-form boys, their responsibility about others restrained themselves. Mrs Veal would have liked Tom to have asserted himself, to have protected her, at least carried out a few crates ; but he said he neither felt cut out for the part nor wished to make her seem conspicuous, and sat now in her sitting-room holding an empty whisky-glass, waiting with little patience for her to come and fill it.

When at last she came, rather crossly : " I am not cut out to do noble things," he said. " It always makes me feel vaguely uneasy."

He was sliding away from her, away from everyone, she knew. They had reached a frightening hiatus the evening before. Alone in the sitting-room, he had suddenly gone over to the mantelpiece, slipped a half-crown from the middle of a pile of silver and dropped it quietly in his pocket. She was always leaving little heaps of money about and it had seemed unlikely that she would ever notice ; but she had, had flicked at him a little terrified glance as if she herself had been caught out, had flushed in misery and shame. He was sorry for her, but looked back blandly, could not have cared less.

"What does 'Etreinte' mean?" she asked now, sniffing at some perfume one of the travellers had brought. She read the name with a fancy accent off the box.

"It means a death-grapple," he said, smiling.

She held the scented palm of her hand before his face.

'Men and women,' he thought. 'In that close and violent contention, how isolated is the soul, how frozen in space, how pitifully solitary, since only the limbs fight, the nerves reply, the blood warms and runs and illuminates, the flesh argues. The soul is afar off, beyond the other's shoulder, very still, like a star.'

"I think I want to get away from here," he said.

"Here?"

"The village, the house, here, Marion."

"Yet you can't?"

"Too lazy."

"No. Not that reason." She closed her eyes and covered her face with her scented hands.

"Because it's easier sponging on Marion," he said, stretching, yawning.

"No. Not the money, either."

"Then because why?" He turned to her, a little surprised, and after a while she took her hands from her face and said: "Because there is someone you must stay near."

Silence dropped over the room like a glass dome. They seemed frozen. Her hands seemed so lifeless that she could not even cover her face again.

.   .   .   .   .

Tinty climbed into the full-up and shuddering bus in the market-place, in her basket the rennet, the vinegar, the double-satin ribbon, and in her heart words of whole pure bliss. She tasted her happiness slowly, as if it were a comforting drink to sip. The bus lurched forward and she swung with it, holding the strap, feeling her body light and taut as a girl's. Odd that such a nondescript man held the keys for her into such healing peace: a stranger, a man she had never even been introduced to, yet he could put her at rest with a few words.

And now the bus, with the swarming tea-time streets behind, began to blind its way through high hedgerowed lanes. She rocked, swayed, hanging by one hand. " Sound as a bell." The words were whole, perfect. She said them to herself until they rang in her ears exultantly.

A little tapping on her elbow was quite an elderly bald-headed man struggling to have her attention, to get to his feet and give her his seat. She smiled, she was gay, shaking her head (for there was not room for the commotion of it all and two or three miles is nothing). But he insisted. There he was on his feet now, easy, like a sailor, with the bus swaying and swinging. She sat down, smiled again and this time nodded, but a little shadow had crossed her face. Had she not detected there in *his* face, too, a shadow of concern?

  .   .   .   .   .

When Tinty arrived home the others were sitting by opened windows looking at photograph-albums. The air seemed heavy and the park was hushed, the trees strangely lucid against the mulberry sky.

" It will be a pity if there's a storm," said Tinty, easing her feet in her shoes, sinking into Marion's chair. " That field the other side of 'The Blacksmith's Arms', I noticed from the bus—a very heavy crop of wheat." She was town-bred and liked talking in this way.

" It's oats beyond 'The Blacksmith's Arms'," said Margaret.

" It was not pale enough for oats, and it hadn't that shimmer on it," said Tinty, going back to her town talk.

"All the same, it's oats." Margaret laughed carelessly to show she thought the matter trivial, but added: "Isn't it, Marion?"

Marion shrugged. "The squirrels feel the storm coming," he said, standing at the window, looking out at the trees and the flashes of grey, plunging, rippling in the branches.

Margaret turned over a photograph-album in a huff, glancing with scorn at relations with babies, bouquets or croquet-mallets. Marion irritated her. It was only through hearing him speak of the oats that she *knew* . . . not that it mattered . . . but it was so typical . . .

Sophy ran from shoulder to shoulder, explaining.

"Don't lean over and breathe so," said Margaret. "Did you get the ribbon, mother? You look done in. It was silly not to let me take the car."

"Yes, here it is, dear. How fusty those albums smell."

"Everything in the library smells like that," said Sophy.

"One day," Marion said to Cassandra, "we must really go through the library. Weed out and catalogue and do some repair work."

She looked up from the album of Marion's aunts and uncles and smiled.

"Perhaps to-night," he even suggested, shocked at his own decision, the sudden wish to work.

"Oh, mother, I said *cream*," Margaret cried. "*Not* white."

"And this," said Sophy, giggling, her arms round Cassandra's neck, "is Uncle Charles by the monkey-puzzle."

"Sophy, it's bedtime," said Tinty.

"Oh, *must* I. . . .?"

"Of course you must."

"Sophy!"

"Yes, father?"

"Don't fling out of the room like that. Say good night.

122

No, of course you couldn't do it graciously now. But another time."

Margaret was sulky still. She took up another of the albums and turned the stiff pages rapidly. "Ah, here is Marion in his hey-day," she said spitefully. "Age has not withered him . . ."

No one heard, for Tom burst in, waving some book of Sophy's. "Marion, look!" he cried. "In the conservatory! I found it just now. How many more times do I need to warn you about it? Don't you care? Or can't you control your child? Does she just defy you? Cassandra, where *is* she? Where is Sophy now?"

"She has gone to bed," Marion said.

No one spoke for a moment and then Tinty sighed and said: "Well!" and, putting both hands on the arms of her chair, eased herself up, like an old woman, scattering her parcels, fussing. Cassandra was ill-at-ease. She had been staring at Uncle Charles by the monkey-puzzle for quite five minutes.

CHAPTER TWELVE

THE SKY looked swollen, as if it held some darker, heavier substance than rain, as if at a finger's pressure it would let down a stained syrup, like the blackberry juice dripping from the muslin net in the kitchen.

" Leave it be ! " said Nanny.

Mrs Adams put down the purple wooden spoon.

" Let's have a clear jelly for heaven's sake. We can't hasten Nature,"

Cassandra came in and there was a stubborn silence. " I want to make some paste . . ." she began. " Just flour and water . . ."

" Paste ? " said Nanny vaguely, as if she had never spent all those wet afternoons with different generations of children and their scrap-books and the jelly-like stuff in a basin.

" For some books in the library."

" Well, you're welcome to what you can find, of course. I've got me blackberry-jam to get on with directly and Mrs Adams here's got one of her queer turns . . ."

" That's right," said Mrs Adams.

They watched in silence while Cassandra mixed the paste and carried it away.

" Did you notice her flushing ? " Nanny began. " Quiet as a mouse, but I size her up all right."

" What're you going to do ? "

" I shall speak to him."

" I should," said Mrs Adams, standing the milk in water and draping it with cheese-cloth. Her face was drawn. She pressed her fist into the small of her back.

"This weather's curdled your stomach," said Nanny—one of her kind impulses.

"I feel at the end of me tether."

Out in the yard there was a sudden rustle of leaves.

"Wind springing up," they said in the kitchen.

.　　　.　　　.　　　.　　　.

The trees seemed smothered in their own foliage, the wind bore the branches down, ruffling them and turning up the whiter undersides of the leaves. Just as it was growing dark the lights fused on the ground-floor of the house, and in the library Marion was obliged to hold aloft a large branched candlestick as they went along the shelves.

"This corner by the fireplace Violet and I did years ago," he explained. "Mostly old books on anatomy and eighteenth-century cookery-books. When she—when we had done that lot we seemed to lose heart."

Candle-grease slanted on to the floor-boards and hardened opaquely. They opened bird-books, some of them exotic birds from other lands, lyre-birds, parrots and macaws, toucans, the great bird-of-paradise, their plumage beautifully engraved; or books with coloured plates of fruit, rough-skinned brown pears and red-streaked apples, mulberries, quinces, medlars. A grey mould lay on all the books, leather had peeled away and the pages were stippled with little freckles.

Suddenly there was a loud tap at the door, an insulting pause, and Nanny came in.

"Could I speak to you, sir?"

He lowered the candlestick and brought her into the wavering light.

"Of course."

She waited, looking at Cassandra.

"We are busy, as you see. What do you want?"

" Only to speak to you, sir."

" Please . . ." Cassandra began, stepping forward, dropping books from her arms as she did so.

" All right ! "

Marion put the candlestick on the table and went quickly into the hall.

When she was alone, Cassandra sat down at the table and looked through the books, trying to read a little, but the room with its shadows, its long windows, the light which drew grey furry moths in from outside, excited her, enchanted her. It seemed to be an evening quite separate from any other. The crumbling books on the table before her seemed like books which had never been read ; dust encrusted what had once been gilded edges ; in some there were faint signatures, a pressed brown violet, yellowed newspaper-cuttings ; a jay's feather fell out of one, a dead spider from another. Yet the books themselves seemed clenched together, as if the pages had never been turned.

Lightning ran over the sky behind the monkey-puzzle tree and, when the thunder followed she thought of the conservatory, waiting for the avalanche of shattered glass which any vibration might begin.

When Marion came back he was laughing. He had despatched Nanny, confounded, as no one else could have done. She had been up against his goodness, which had not allowed her to insinuate.

Cassandra's hair was like a piece of silk in the candlelight. He ran his hand over it and under her chin.

" Sophy's birthday soon," he began, moving away from her and walking up and down. " Shall we give her another Siamese cat, or would that be an obtuse thing to do ? "

" No. No, I don't think so."

" Poor Nanny had lost a two-shilling piece. She says it is the principle of the thing. Now she has gone back to veil the mirrors and pictures—on account of the lightning, d'you see? Cassandra, what is wrong?"

She sat with her head bent over the books.

"Look at me!"

She shook her head.

"All these dirty books have depressed you. Your eyes are tired with so many 'f's and 's's. Put your palms over them—no, not touching!—relax until there is only darkness. What do you see? Flowers, stars and suns? Your hands are too small." (For she had covered her face quickly.) "Don't touch your eyelids." He stood behind her and cupped his hands over the hollowed bone, so that no crack or glimmer of light could enter. "Now what do you see? Peacocks' feathers? Nothing at all?"

She saw his face clearly against the darkness.

"I see—nothing," she said.

A tear dropped into his hand and ran down his wrist, he felt her lashes wet against his palms.

He turned her to face him, lifted the candelabrum and searched her face with concern. She tried to cover her eyes with her spread fingers, but tears gathered and ran down between them. At last she gave in, looked up at him, waiting for whatever he would say. She made no sound and scarcely breathed, yet her face was wet and bruised like a flower in the rain.

"My sweet Cassandra!"

Still holding the candles high, he drew her closer to him and kissed her. She received his kiss, but did not return it, for she did not know how, nor did it occur to her, so netted up in bliss was she, so content to be held by him, not stirring, heedless of the next day and the next minute.

Marion was happy, too, without knowing or wondering why.

.   .   .   .   .

"How typical!" cried Margaret. "A houseful of young men and no one can mend a fuse."

"There are only Tom and Marion," said her mother, "and Tom is out, and it is not the sort of thing Marion could do. Adams has gone to look for some fuse wire."

Margaret folded her hands on what remained of her lap and closed her eyes. 'Oh, Ben!' she thought. 'How I miss you! You would have had the house ablaze with light *ages* ago.'

'She only misses her husband,' Tinty thought, counting stitches by the lamplight. 'Any young woman would be the same.' The smell of the burning wick took her back many years. The light grew up unevenly in a blue crown and she lowered it a little.

.   .   .   .   .

'*Fork* lightning!' thought Nanny, putting scissors and knives quickly into the dresser drawer. She took up her stand away from the window, thinking of young Mr Tom as a boy. What a bad example he had set Miss Violet's brothers when he came to stay. He was as bold as brass. Running out into the garden under the lightning. She could put no fear into him. Try as she might. And Miss Violet had stood at the window clapping her hands, calling and laughing. The long rain came suddenly down, sticking his fringe close to his forehead, swamping his sailor-blouse, as he capered about on the lawn. . . . That evening she went to Madam. . . .

.   .   .   .   .

Tom cut across the park homewards, past the ruin in which a hermit had once lived, paid by eighteenth-century Vanbrughs a few shillings a week and board to dwell there and wander picturesquely against the background of the woods in grey robes. Tom had often liked to imagine him on his evening off (for surely he had had one), his robe left on its hook above the ancient Hebrew tome (he could not, Tom thought, read his own language, let alone another), sitting in the tap-room of "The Blacksmith's Arms" amusing the villagers with the follies of the gentry, how it was a carefree life and easy, but monotonous. He could not know how precarious his living was; but the Gothic vogue would pass as the Chinese had, and the dead fir trees so carefully planted beside his hermitage would soon be as uninteresting as the overgrown pagodas in the shrubbery.

It was growing dark and the waste, bleached grass rising up on his right, and the blood-red sorrel, stood against the pigeon-coloured sky, curiously still. Yet as he went through the churchyard the wind began to whip through his hair. On Violet's grave the rose-bush had no blossom to offer. In a jar was a bunch of scabious and Queen-Anne's-Lace. He seemed to see with such clear outline that he might have drawn it, the picture of the earth on which he walked, the various strata—gravel, chalk, clay—and in one layer the little chambers of death, the boxes of bones lying in rows and, placed grotesquely in one of them, indistinguishable from, say, 'Hannah Bracewell aged 49', he thought, passing some very black lettering on granite, lay *his* Violet with her beauty quite vanished, none of it left anywhere in the world (he pushed through the lych-gate—'the corpse-gate' he thought), his memories of it even hardening into mere symbols. A large spot of rain fell on his hand, but he did not walk more quickly, going now up the lime avenue, tented in by leaves. Haunted, this place was, Nanny said and Sophy said, since those who have not fears enough will invent some.

At the end of the avenue was the walled-in garden and he went in and walked round a little in the warmth, felt in the darkness for a ripe fig, thrusting his hand into the leaves for the ribbed fruit, grazing his knuckles against the warm bricks, walked up and down the paths eating. The churchyard: the walled-in garden—the two sides of himself. As the rain increased, the smell that rose up from the earth and the box-hedging and the nail-pitted bricks was heady and overwhelming. When the thunder came it reminded him of the conservatory and he went quickly towards the house, crossing the lawn in haste.

Lights fell from the façade, blanching the two broken goddesses on either side of the steps—Flora and Pomona, with their chipped fruit and garlands and the crumbling nymphs along the terrace.

The rain fell all over the conservatory, as rapid as machine-gun fire, the palm clashed its leaves together in the draught. Tom walked right round, peering in through the cobwebbed glass, and then, suddenly conscious of the rain and his wet clothes, turned up his collar and with his hands in his pockets began to trot briskly, head down against the rain, towards the kitchen door.

As he went in through the bakehouse Adams came out with a sack over his head and a carpenter's bag in his hand. He thrust his head out of the sack, turning it to left and right, like a tortoise, and then, satisfied that the rain could not be heavier, plunged out into the darkness.

Nanny sat alone in the kitchen with a bowl of sloes in her lap, pricking them with a darning needle, for gin. The juice spurted out over her stained fingers. Tom stood stamping his wet feet on the doormat.

" Shake that jacket in the bakehouse," she said sharply.

When he came back in his shirt-sleeves, he asked : " What was Adams doing here so late? "

" The electric fused. Hang your jacket on the airer for a bit. It's gone right through your shirt. Take the roller-towel and give your hair a rub."

Murmuring and cursing, she put down the basin of sloes

and went into the scullery. When she came back she had a bowl of frothy, hot mustard-water.

"Get your shoes off and your feet into that."

"Oh, Nanny, don't act so silly." 'Is she in her second childhood?' he wondered. 'Or does she think I am in mine?' But he did as he was told, which was more than he would have done as a little boy, she thought, watching him rolling up his trousers, stripping off his wet socks. The imprint of ribbed knitting was on his cold feet. Tinty always made his socks too thick.

"My God, it's hot!"

She sat calmly in her chair again, ignoring him.

"You know, it's very comforting. I had quite forgotten. How wonderful it is, being a child—sitting there with your feet in hot water, eating bread-and-milk and the smell of clothes scorching on the fire-guard."

"The only thing I ever scorched was one of Miss Violet's holland smocks. I didn't know how to go to Madam. It was one she had worked herself. Miss Violet set herself off into one of her tantrums, of course."

"What did you do about that?" Tom asked, his arms folded across his chest.

"Sponged her face with cold water. She wasn't easy to deal with. Even up till the last, when she was expecting. I remember when I was doing her hair one night and I found a white hair at the back. Not that it means anything at the back. If it's going white for good it begins at the temples. 'Well, Miss Violet . . . Well, Madam!' I said. I pulled the hair out and showed it to her in the palm of me hand. She looks at it for a moment, then she falls forward on her arms across the dressing-table, thumping with her fists all among the glass bottles and sobbing! I give her a good slapping."

Tom lifted a pink crinkled foot out of the water and examined it. "It feels dead."

Overhead the thunder seemed to splinter across the roof-top.

"Is that half-full yet?" she asked, holding up the bottle with its layers of berries.

"Not quite," he lied. "Go on telling me about her." He fed on her memories. They seemed more vivid than his own.

The rocking-chair tilted back and forth. "'Nanny!' she says to me one morning. 'I've got a flea! I'm bitten all round the waist.' She was, too. I must say, it looked like a flea. I spread out some of my clean drawer paper over her bedroom floor and I stood her on that and stripped her, keeping a close watch all the time, turning all her clothes inside out, shaking them over the paper. She put her head down and ruffled her hair. Laugh!"

Cassandra came in. When she saw Tom sitting there with his trousers rolled up, his hair untidy, his feet soaking, she drew back in confusion.

"That water's no good to you now," said Nanny, handing him the towel.

"I wanted some warm milk for Sophy," said Cassandra. "The storm has frightened her. Please don't move. I can find the pan and heat it."

"I expect it's gone sour," said Nanny. "Mrs Adams did her best with it. We ought to have one of them 'frig's. These houses are all swank at the front and inconvenience at the back. If I had babies in the house I'd stand out for one—milk turning overnight and green spots on the blackcurrant puree."

"What happened about the flea?" Tom asked.

"I never said anything about no flea," Nanny said, frowning, as Cassandra came back into the kitchen with the milk.

'She gets to be more of a person,' Tom thought, drying his feet quickly, thinking of Cassandra.

When she had gone, Nanny said: "Always running in and out. 'Can I have some paste?' 'Can I have some hot milk?' Any excuse to get into this kitchen."

"Why should she want to come into the kitchen?"

"You've got something there," she said; sinister, if meaningless.

Her insinuations failed with Tom also, for he began to laugh.

"Is that how they talk at the cinema?"

"Some do. Some don't."

"Don't they ever have Greta Garbo now?"

"A rumour here and there. Nothing comes of it. Not that I'm worried."

"Her beauty was moving."

"Them legs!"

"She was the only one who ever made me cry."

"There's a pair of dry socks on the airer." She was pouring gin over the berries in the bottle, which now seemed to lie under a curious light.

"What really happened about the flea?" he asked before he went out of the kitchen.

"We never found it," she said, pressing in the cork of the gin bottle.

.   .   .   .   .

Tom went at once, in his stockinged feet, to Sophy's room. Cassandra sat by the bed palely illuminated by a nightlight in a white saucer: the flame dipped and wavered uncertainly and her shadow reached high and then receded.

She put her hand up and smiled. Once more Sophy lay asleep.

Tom stood at the end of the bed and looked at her.

"What is this?" he whispered taking up an exercise-book from the eiderdown. He read:

133

" She is writing a novel," said Cassandra.

"Good Lord!" He felt it was the last straw.

Cassandra got up stealthily. Her eyes, he thought, looked brilliant, over-ripe with tears.

On the landing he said: " You have never seen my drawings of—of her mother. I once promised to show them to you."

She turned her head away.

" Are you tired? "

" Yes." To keep her evening's happiness intact she knew that she must quickly escape from Tom and his drawings.

But he was beginning to be interested in her and to see for the first time that her innocence was not only a negative attribute and her integrity not merely priggishness.

" Then to-morrow? "

She looked at him with a smile of relief which was quite incomprehensible to him.

" Yes, to-morrow."

For between this day and the next was there not a whole long night of counting the measure of her wealth, a few phrases, a touch, a kiss and, for the first time, the circle of her existence approached and cut across by another's, the loneliness dispelled and the imprisoning darkness routed; surely, for ever? When we are young, we imagine the circles one day becoming concentric and many other strange fantasies concerning the human personality. At twenty, only death threatens. And that from so afar.

She went into her room and flung up the window from the bottom and leant out into the cool rainy darkness. The rose-garden was like a tangle of ink-scrawls. The storm had been drawn away across a ridge of hills and now the rain dropped with steady concentration, striking into the foliage and the roots of grass, falling impartially over graves in the churchyard and the goddesses before the house.

Cassandra read her page of Shakespeare, but she had been reading the same page for some weeks.

.   .   .   .   .

In Tom's room Bony was sitting in his corner reading a book. Sophy had arranged him like that for a little joke before going to bed. Tom took *Ben Hur* from Bony's pelvic basin and went to the window.

He was still thinking of Cassandra. 'To-morrow,' he thought, picking up a pen and a scrap of paper. He drew for a little while and then went to bed. Then the house was engulfed in darkness, only Marion's windows still shedding a faint light down over the wet terrace.

CHAPTER THIRTEEN

CASSANDRA, waking in the morning, felt her heart race away from her to greet the day. The sky was grey and blue, watery like a child's painting of clouds, and chalk-white birds dropped and glided against it. She lay and watched them, her hands clasped between head and pillow.

She was half-reluctant to meet Marion at breakfast, wishing to spin out her happiness, to have it all smooth and without confusion, her delight woven slowly and flawlessly. And she was shy. 'I shall be as if nothing has happened,' she thought in her innocence. 'I shall be quiet. I shall say nothing.' (She seldom said anything and had never been noisy.) 'And how will he confront me?' she wondered. 'How will he speak to me about the storm, ask whether I slept or not, will I have marmalade or honey, without betraying to the others how I am changed, so that I can never go back to what I was yesterday or ever again be without those words "My sweet Cassandra" to keep me company?'

Her thoughts about breakfast-time were suddenly swept aside by the reality of the little candlelit scene which she had brought, menaced at one point by Tom, to bed and lain with last night and wakened to this morning—the clear and sensuous memory of being near to him, of tears drying stiffly upon her face as he kissed her, of the rain beating down outside and the smell of candles burning unevenly in the great musty room.

Although she allowed herself to think no further ahead than breakfast-time, she was troubled and impatient when the image of the night before cut into her plans, and her head moved on the pillow, her eyes quickly closing and her profile turned sharply against her crooked elbow. Only after the vision had grown less certain could she relax and open her eyes again to the windowful of blue and grey clouds and the floating birds. And presently got up and dressed, tensely rehearsing before the mirror the look she would wear for breakfast. 'It has happened to me,' she thought, combing her hair away from her temples. 'Love has happened to me.' And she laid down the comb and moving stiffly as if she were frozen went downstairs.

Marion awoke, but kept his eyes closed. Pain pursued him from his dream into the daylight. Presently, he got up and dressed slowly and went downstairs, down the dark core of the lulled and shadowy house. In the hall was Sophy's book which Tom had thrown down in his fit of temper the night before, *The Pluckiest Girl in the School*. Tom had given it to her, no doubt. Marion most certainly had not.

A gentle chinking of crockery came from the kitchen as he went down the flagged passage. The kitchen cat crunched her teeth into a dead rat, growled at Marion from behind it, her eyes slit, a white paw laid over her prize.

In the kitchen Nanny was drinking tea. She wore the padded crimson dressing-gown which had been the first glimpse of the morning to so many little children. So often, too, she had appeared in it to young mothers, as she creaked in with their babies at daybreak. Stirring on their pillows, heavy with milk, at five-to-six, they had opened their eyes upon that dressing-gown with its quilted diamonds, and Nanny, with the two thin plaits over her shoulders as now, had watched her moving sternly as a priestess, handing over the sacred object as if she had kept vigil all night while they, the fruitful, the indolent and heedless, had slept. Even now, to Marion, she gave the impression of having kept her wits about her all night.

" What's got you up? " she asked, her eyes suspicious over

the steaming cup. " One of these days I'll get to the bottom of this everlasting trapesing into my kitchen." Then flushed, having spoken as if she were a cook. ' My kitchen, indeed! ' When you get into a slack household you lose grip of your pride.

" You think *I* am after the baker's change now," he said. He chose a nice cup off the dresser and held it out for tea.

" You'll have to have the ordinary milk. The condensed's finished. It's not like you drinking tea."

" I'm going out. I shan't be in for breakfast."

She couldn't remember when he had last left the grounds. A little walk in the park, down to the ice-house and back, or along the haunted avenue, but he never went beyond, never into the village, perhaps once or twice a year to London to a dentist, nothing more. She was a little disturbed, as she had all her life been disturbed by anything out of the ordinary. The monotony of nursery life seemed to be still the rhythm which she desired, that routine where only the abnormal is to be feared, where all disturbances, even red-letter days (the birthday, the pantomime, the half-term holiday) are better over. (" You'll end up in tears." " I'm afraid they're unsettled, madam.")

" I thought that milk had turned." She watched him skimming the white flecks off with his spoon. " I wonder we don't have a 'frig."

He could not bear to be bothered about the house. His look of distaste and weariness reassured her, as sudden acquiescence or enthusiasm would not have done. Still testing him, she went on : " Miss Sophy got off all right in the end, then ? Last night, I mean."

" Was there any trouble ? "

" There was plenty of trouble *made*. Miss Dashwood up and downstairs with hot milk. The storm frightened her, they said."

138

" They? "

" Her and Mr Tom. They sat up with her till late. When I heard them whispering on the landing I took it she was O.K. More tea? "

" No more."

He sat too still for her liking. " She's highly strung, that child. Takes things to heart. Mrs Courage's girl was the same until they packed her off to school. The Young Ladies' Cheltenham College. She came back quite different."

" I don't want Sophy different," he said, guessing the tenor of her words.

" What would her mother have said, I wonder? "

" Her mother never went to school."

(' You're telling me! ' she said to herself grimly in an American accent.) Aloud, she said : " But she was different. There will never be another to hold a candle to *her*."

" No." He still sat very quietly by the window.

' That sunk in,' she thought.

But nothing could sink into his mind this morning. A layer of pain interposed, absorbing and destroying each new idea. He could not even make a decision about a refrigerator, let alone search into the remote corners of his heart, analyse his inclinations and put past and future upon scales and come to a conclusion about the result.

He left his tea and went out of the kitchen and across the courtyard, putting himself out of Cassandra's reach and out of reach of Nanny's darting, insinuating tongue.

The garden was brilliant, drenched. Roses like sodden, crushed up paper hung against the stable walls, the stones across the yard were washed clean and little cascades of rain were shaken from the lime trees. Down the lane, rivulets of wet sand crossed and recrossed one another and brown bubbled water hastened still into an occasional drain. At the turn of the lane the whole valley lay exposed. The rain-beaten corn stretched away in great wet swathes as if it were cut and strewn and piled across the fields, with the unevenness of a desert after a sandstorm, undulating, blown and chaotic. Like a great painting of corn, he thought, resting his leather-patched elbows on a gate. The oats beyond "The Black-smith's Arms" had fared worst of all. Tinty would certainly have seen no shimmer upon it this morning, he decided.

That moment, that argument the evening before came back to him, puzzled him. The storm brooding over the land-scape had perhaps given to the scene its air of unreality, as if what they said (Tinty and Margaret bickering about crops, Sophy trying to draw their attention away from her bedtime) was only the outward and visible sign of an inward, invisible crisis, a crisis in the tension and compulsion of their lives together. "*Cream* ribbon, not white," Margaret had said. And rejected her mother, who sat like an old woman with her hands useless in her lap. He, himself, turning from the window had suddenly looked across at Cassandra and said, his own voice surprising him : " One day, we must go through the library," as if he were really saying: " Will you marry me?" She had looked up from her photograph-album and smiled, saying " Yes." But Tom had broken in upon them, flinging down Sophy's book, raising his voice. What mean-ing had that, Marion wondered? None that he could see. For Tom was outside the stresses and compulsions of human intercourse.

Marion walked on down towards the shallow hollow where the pub stood with its untidy outbuildings. In the yard, Gilbert's turkeys turned from his approach with the false, prodigious dignity of camels, going away towards a patch of nettles, with a dipping, spondaic movement, as if they went by clockwork, swans going across a backcloth. As he stood watching them, the pub door opened and he saw a pink-kimona'd arm reaching for the milk bottle. He moved away from the turkeys and, as he crossed the square of gravel in front of the pub, the woman drew back, although staring at him. Before she kicked the door to with a feathered shoe, he had glimpsed the hair coiled and pinned under a net, the grey stork embroidered on her wrap, and he remembered the one-sided conversation he had had with Margaret some time before. Perhaps this was the very woman who had disturbed her so on Tom's account. Even remembering Violet, as he walked on down the road, he was not surprised, still less shocked, for he perceived that when we lose the best, we do not always try for the second-best, but often the very worst of all. At least that is kinder to the second-best, he thought, seeing Cassandra's face with tears upon it.

His head felt as if someone were doing knitting in it. Nothing was simple. He believed that he loved Cassandra tenderly; but marriage is not simple. It brought with it, Nanny had reminded him, so many complications which were beyond his energies. Tinty stood before him, and Tom, Nanny with her talk of refrigerators and change, the thought of beginning a new life in that fast-crumbling house, of leaving a mouldering and rank corner of earth to sons, perhaps, and then engaging servants, spending money, laying down wine, planting and clearing. In the library last night, no one, nothing had stood between him and Cassandra. Now so much interposed. She was a child merely, to be led into so dark, so lonely a wilderness as his heart. For her, so much unravelling of people, so much sorting out of possessions would have to be done. He might draw her to him and ease the passion which lay under her silence, lead her into the circle of ice which encompassed him : but the obstacles were still outside, where the world was, and even within him, there was Violet.

.   .   .   .   .   .

Cassandra had sat through breakfast, stunned and wounded. Now, in the schoolroom, dictating French to Sophy, she knew that he was avoiding her, that an intolerable situation had come about, which she could end only, she was thinking, by going away. She felt like closing the book there, in the middle of a sentence, and running out of the house, for his sake and her own.

"*Il y a.* ..."

"What again?" asked Sophy sharply.

"Again?"

"You said it once before."

"Oh! No, only once. *Le plaisir.* ..."

She clasped her hands behind her chair, tightly, for Sophy's heavy breathing, as she worked, plucked at her nerves.

Sophy wrote slowly in an unfamiliar hand, Greek 'e's, German 'f 's and various other affectations, which she thought would look well one day in the British Museum, or in biographies—a facsimile of the author's handwriting.

"*Comme un grand frisson* ..." Cassandra went on. "Sophy, I will not have those 'f 's."

The child looked up blankly.

"Can't you hear what I am saying?"

"Yes."

('Oh, God, give me patience!' Cassandra prayed. 'When and how do I go? And where?') "Write as your father taught you. Don't show off."

Sophy tried to convey the impression that all her liberties were infringed, the very expression of her individuality stripped from her and forbidden.

Cassandra had never spoken sharply before. She looked at her with new interest and resumed her writing reluctantly as the dictation began again ... "*un grand frisson et* ..."

"*Un grand* what?"

"'*Frisson.*' You are supposed to have prepared this."

142

" Oh, I thought it *ought* to be ' *frisson* ', but you seemed to be saying something different." ('Two can play this game,' she thought.)

Cassandra, who avoided speaking French in front of Marion, because she knew her accent was that of the English schoolgirl, blushed and then asked firmly, but too late: "What did you think I said?"

" ' *Poisson*,' " said Sophy, her face so clear, so candid. She could not celebrate her little victory, but liked it none the less. "*Comme un grand poisson.* That was what I *thought* I heard."

.   .   .   .   .

Marion had walked right down the valley and now came up through the woods towards the park. The clouds lumbered by like pieces of torn scenery giving the sun a chance here and there. Perhaps the sun coming out, the earth bracing itself, or perhaps that sight, earlier, of Mrs Veal, had changed him. Whatever it had been, he began to walk quickly, even though the pain still wheeled around his eye-socket. He walked up through the beech-trees, stumbling on the white flints which lay like half-buried bones among the moss.

Sometimes, a small thing, the way words are arranged, or the sun striking the flesh, as it struck his hands now, will set one's blood tingling and one's life on a fresh course.

His steps quickened with his decision, as if he were afraid that a few seconds would alter everything.

It was long after breakfast. She would be sitting at the schoolroom table with Sophy. Her face would be turned towards him as he opened the door. She would smile. But there he checked himself, knowing that, while Sophy was there, he could not speak to her. He would walk over and stand by the window, looking out over the courtyard and listening to Cassandra's patient explanations. It was remarkable how she always remained gentle, no matter how obtuse Sophy managed to be. Violet could never have been so patient. He frowned. Was he to stoop to comparing the living with the dead? And to the detriment of the dead. He had never censured Violet in his mind before, although he had sympathised with her weaknesses.

In the schoolroom, what were they doing now? He imagined Sophy drawing circles with her compasses which always wobbled and skidded so that the two ends of the circle would never meet: or halving the smudged pear-shaped Africa with a slanting equator; or writing one of her essays— "The Death of Chatterton" or "Shelley's Funeral Pyre". Every essay-subject could be made to embrace some harrowing scene, and Mary Stuart or Keats or Kit Marlowe would make their sudden appearance in 'What I Should Like to be When I grow Up' or 'My Favourite Walk.'

Just before lunch he would ask Cassandra to walk on the terrace with him. He leant on a stile at the edge of the wood, waiting for the time to pass, and watching the birds bursting out of the hedges and a large striped spider sitting on a webbed bramble, drawing blood from a fly neatly and methodically. 'We will walk up and down the terrace,' he thought. ' I will ask her to marry me, and she will say " yes." '

A skein of wild geese flew above the trees, with a steady commotion of wings beating, their necks stretched forward into the distance which they desired and made for. He watched them flying over until they were gone beyond the trees, and felt that they crowned his intention, those strange and beautiful birds.

.   .   .   .   .

Mrs Veal, stepping out of her bath, had a Rubens magnificence. Her little rosy knees looked lost under the great massing thighs. One curve of flesh ran into another. Although Rubens might have delighted in her luxuriance, she did not delight in it herself and was soon braced into a different shape, the curves at least separated from one another, if they could not be flattened out.

While she was dressing, her mind remained blank. She went through the complicated ritual of hair-pinning, rouge-ing and powdering, deft work with dark pencils and mascara, as if she were going on to the stage at Drury Lane instead of the Saloon Bar of a village pub. Stretching her mouth and eyes wide, she painted her fair lashes with a little brush. She tried a little dab of the new perfume inside her wrist, sniffed it, rubbed her two wrists together and thrust her scented fingers into her hair. When she had done all this, her mind began to tick over once more and, going downstairs, she mused upon Marion whom she saw so seldom that she had scarcely recognised him. She could not be said to dislike any kind of man, but he was certainly the kind she liked least, deploring his effeminacy in a self-deluding way, knowing without acknowledging the fact that he would never put himself within her scope. She was, all the same, a little inquisitive about him, and when Tom came into the bar mentioned Marion's early morning walk. As she talked, she lifted glasses and dusted the shelves beneath them. Tom said nothing, even pulled round a newspaper so that he could see the headlines.

She could never imagine life up at the Big House, as she called it to herself, could have pictured grandeur but could find no standard for the lives they led, met as she so contin-ually was by hints of dilapidation, of servants giving orders to employers, of discomforts and shabbiness, which she her-self could not have endured. On the other hand, Adams in the public bar would speak of carrying in nectarines for breakfast, and how half a tree might burn in the hall and ones hands remain red with cold. And until recently a watch-maker from the village made regular journeys to wind and

145

adjust all the different clocks, going from room to room; and had described the great wreathed carpets and the stained glass at a hall window with foreign words and a coat-of-arms, and how dust lay in the carved wood and a dark tapestry covered a whole wall, only a pale hand and face and a milk-white deer discernible. But now he went there no more; perhaps all the clocks were silent with their hands at different angles.

Mrs Veal was gratified by the nectarines going in for breakfast, as if she were to eat them herself, and had accompanied the watchmaker from room to room in her imagination, unfolded her table-napkin, thick as a board, before displays of Georgian silver, of pink roses.

But next day, Tom would destroy her pieced-together picture, saying he refused to bath, it unnerved him and the water was always cold, or that Nanny would not let them have a fire in the dining-room. And the evening meal was supper merely, and Tinty sat at it in a tweed coat.

Tom had made up his mind this morning to have two whiskies and go. Before lunch he meant to show his drawings to Cassandra, since she had so strangely refused to see them the night before.

Mrs Veal tried not to sense his abstraction, but her week of freedom from her husband, so long anticipated, had become dull and lonely. She even wished Gilbert back.

"A nice grilled chop for lunch?" she suggested. "Is that a good idea?" And awaited his next cruelty.

"I'm not staying down. I'm going in a minute."

She smiled gallantly, controlling her trembling lips. It was the worst thing she could have done. Tom could not bear stoicism in those he hurt, could not bear the guilt of forcing them into such courage. Marion's refusal, as a boy, to be broken had increased Tom's savagery; now, he yawned, glanced at the clock and stood up.

" Cassandra will be waiting."

She said nothing.

"Sophy's birthday is soon. Cassandra is coming with me to buy her a present. I thought of giving her a Siamese cat." The last part was true, for he had once thought of it. The idea had flashed through his mind, fast pursued by the knowledge that he would never have enough money to spare.

"When shall I see you?" she asked lightly.

"Oh, some time, some time!" He dropped his hat on to the back of his head and sauntered out.

Tears rolled into her eyes.

Tom had nothing to do now. He hissed spitefully at the turkeys as he passed and they scattered in a flurry of panic-stricken hauteur. Why had Marion disappeared, he wondered.

The bus lurched into the square before the pub, turned in the loose gravel and stood palpitating while one or two people stepped down. Tom wondered if he should go into the town for a drink. He fingered his money and knew it was not enough.

Thinking of Cassandra, as if she might help him to forget his disappointment, he set off up the hill. 'I am a reformed character,' he told himself. 'Never to be pestered or bored or tortured by that abominable woman again.' The sun coming out appeared to bless and endorse his resolution. 'One whisky!' he marvelled. 'One less than I intended.' ('One less than I could pay for,' he also thought, but could easily answer the cynicism, for obviously a little baby-talk would have given him all the drink he wanted, as it had before.)

At that moment the wild geese flew down the valley and he stopped to watch them beating their way forward, unhesitatingly and in union, keeping to their prearranged hierarchy.

Smoke wound up out of the pub chimney and the village houses seemed painted flatly, as if in tempera, in the milky morning light.

As he approached the house Sophy and Cassandra came out on to the terrace. Cassandra stood listlessly in the sunshine. Sophy was shooing a hen away from the front door, running behind it and clapping her hands, and when Tom whistled she looked up and waved. 'She never has a good romp,' he thought. 'She will grow up sedate and cold-blooded like Cassandra.'

Crossing the lawn, he picked up a wet fir-cone and aimed at her as she stood waving by the balustrade, made little feints at her until she screamed shrilly with delight and excitement. She clasped one of the grey goddesses, her thin arms quick and alive against the rain-pitted stone, her yellow dress fluttering. She swung herself out of his sight, but he could see an edge of yellow dress and hear her laughter.

In a dreamlike way, the statue appeared to move. It reeled drunkenly and Tom stood frozen in a world where things happened beyond his understanding and Cassandra screamed, her hands clapped over her face.

Tom was strong. He soon lifted the bulk of broken stone, but Sophy, of course, was dead.

CHAPTER FOURTEEN

MRS VEAL was in church for the funeral service, sitting behind a pillar at the back, where the family would never see her but where she could watch and criticise. There was plenty to criticise. Firstly, she thought it unsuitable that Margaret should be there at all, especially buttoned up in bottle-green and looking well. Few of them seemed to know how to behave on such an occasion. Tom fidgeted, cast bored looks at the stained-glass window and at his finger-nails; Cassandra looked merely frightened as she had done the first time Mrs Veal saw her, in the train; Tinty wept, but into a pink handkerchief : as for Marion, the paler he was, the more effeminate he looked. Only Nanny redeemed them, her hands clasped, her walk impressive, her sealskin coat so funereal. She was right in her heart and knew how to express those emotions rightly. She mourned. She did not gloss over or, in the modern way, deny publicity to her grief.

Tom thought : ' We have certainly had our fair share of funerals.' This was the second time his better nature had induced him to come and uphold Marion, although he saw no sense in any of it and thought uncivilised all the unnecessary and heartrending funeral-trappings, the pitiful little box with its bronze chrysanthemums and bits of brass. For whose sake was it done? he wondered. Not Sophy's, surely? And was it not prolonged misery to those who deserved best to be considered? Marion, for instance. Why should everything be done to please the old women—his mother so easily weeping, Nanny in her mauve gloves with the black lines on the back and her correct funeral clothes—she even had, she once confided to Tom, correct apparel for her own funeral, a lawn nightgown with valenciennes lace given to her by Violet's mother and so beautiful that she could not bring herself to wear it while she was still alive.

Why do people die so often from funerals? he wondered. Old people tempted out in poor weather bent upon lugubrious pleasures, their resistance lowered by thoughts of mortality, the graveside turf so damp beneath their feet. Not a drink inside them, either. " We shan't go to a funeral smelling of spirits," as Nanny had said. Marion had ignored her and began to pour a whisky for Tom. But he had not drunk for four days, and refused. He felt neither better nor worse for this abstinence, merely lived on a different plane. He thought he would never drink again. Not because of Sophy, not because it mattered; a little, perhaps, to free himself from Mrs Veal and a little, also, because it was too much trouble. He could not be like Marion with a drink here and there for the drink's sake. Marion revered wine, was well on the way, Tom considered, to being an affected fool about it, one of those who use far-fetched adjectives, such as flamboyant, authentic, forthright and so on—(for a few verses of the Psalm, he amused himself inventing other improbable epithets). Whereas I, he continued, call it all ' the booze ' and despise it because it never does what it promises.

The white chrysanthemums were richly curled and green-shadowed. About this time of year they had had the other funeral. Another poor show. Violet would have arranged it better herself. (By moonlight, purple plumes bunched on the horses' heads, the black horses sequinned, glittering under the moon, the narrow carriages plunging down through the steep-sided lanes, a white owl flying above the hearse and, in the blanched churchyard, a gravedigger waiting with a skull in his hand and his spade silver from the flinty soil.)

"Comfort us again now after the time that Thou hast

plagued us: and for the years wherein we have suffered adversity."

'Some hopes!' thought Tom. Marion stood very stiff and straight, the tips of his fingers resting on the pew before him. 'Chief mourner. He is always that,' Tom thought. 'Comfort *him*, he has been plagued enough.' 'Who'll be chief mourner? I, said the Dove, I'll mourn for my love.' The flowers, the coffin, the family waited. For what? So that Saint Paul should set himself questions and then answer them inadequately, inventing dupes to sharpen his wits upon, that contemptible trick of the argumentative. 'I asked a civil question and I expect a civil answer, as Nanny used to say.' Not 'Thou fool!' 'We did not come here to be insulted.' 'I shan't like the bit outside,' he thought, trying to brace himself. 'I didn't like it with Violet. I won't look at Marion. I will look at little Cassandra this time.'

Between two pillars was the tomb of a Lord of the Manor from those times before any Vanbrughs had lived there, when bread was baked in the bakehouse, and the front of the house showed its own skeleton of wood, had no pediment, no frivolities, no eighteenth-century folly, no cumbersome luxury. The effigies lying on the tomb were painted, the features blunted, man and wife stretched side by side, their hands which had once pointed upwards in prayer were broken from the wrists. At the man's feet lay a little curled dog with a face like a lion, and at the woman's feet was a baby criss-crossed with swathing bands. They had died together, leaving no heir. The young man, with his chipped beard and narrow face, had not watched first a wife go into the grave and then his only child. They had been struck down in the medieval way, thought Marion. A plague, perhaps, or the well-water at the end of a hot summer full of visible creatures. The infant had been hastily baptized (it bore the mark of the chrism) and the father had weakly

151

scratched out his instructions for the tomb, the inscription (in Gothic letters, as befits the dead) and, his living hand among the curls of the little dog and tears starting to his eyes in the English fashion when animals are to be parted from—" my little dog . . ." he had perhaps written—his last words . . . Marion turned his thoughts away. He must not be moved, not by a dog dead three hundred years ago. He looked at Cassandra, who waited wretchedly to follow the coffin out of the church, Saint Paul having had his say.

With immeasurable dignity, Nanny lifted a white handkerchief, bordered with grey, and touched one cheekbone, then the other. Tinty snivelled still into the screwed-up pink affair. The next time Nanny would use her handkerchief would be as the earth struck the coffin-lid. Adams's boots rang hollowly over the stone and gratings as he clanked down the aisle.

Cassandra walked with Nanny behind the family. Mrs Veal approved of that. She was smoothing on her gloves, ready to slip out of the South Door, not daring to let Tom see her.

Outside, the sun was like gold dust in the air. Cassandra stood on the clay-daubed turf and tried, by breathing slowly and regularly, to unknot her throat. The living most often remember with a sense of guilt their past relationships with the newly dead and Cassandra could not forget her last hour or so with Sophy, and her own impatience and the hostility which had sprung up between them, like a gust of wind on a calm day. Sophy was the sort of child about whom one felt confidently that a little later on she would become happier, better adjusted, less driven to morbid secrecy. It was always a little later on that it would happen, and it is painful to think of the dead whose future promised what the past had not given.

Mrs Veal was detained in the porch by one of the villagers,

so that she could not see that Marion had taken up his proper place at the head of the grave. When she had shaken off her washerwoman, she hurried down the path, brushing carelessly through the Michaelmas daisies and keeping well out of sight. Out in the lane, Margaret was sitting in a car, waiting. When she saw Mrs Veal, she blew her nose, turning her head away. She was shivery and her nostrils were red and pinched. "I felt as if I had 'flu' coming on," she would say to her mother later. Margaret never had colds like other people—either 'flu' or nothing.

Mrs Veal hastened away down the hill. "Why *did* I come'''" she asked herself, feeling upset and flurried.

Tom stared at his feet steadily, not at Marion, not even at Cassandra. If he raised his eyes at all it was to look across the churchyard, at the yellow leaves turning in the still air and falling over the grass and gravestones. 'In the midst of life we are in death.' He would never allow himself to remember the little caved-in ribs and the stain spreading upon the yellow dress, so 'Where is Margaret?' he quickly asked himself. Had she let herself give in at last, and what excuse would she set forth and elaborate at tea-time—if one *does* have tea after a funeral?

Nanny lifted her handkerchief again and shortly after they began unevenly mumbling the Lord's Prayer. As they came away from the graveside, Marion walked beside Cassandra. He had said nothing to her for days, no word since the evening in the library. Now, looking straight ahead, he said stiffly: "I should like to thank you for all the kindness you gave to Sophy. And to me." He waved his hand before his eyes, brushing away some threads of cobwebs of which the early autumn air seemed full, then he opened the car door and very civilly bade her get in.

At tea, Margaret drank warm milk. "The draughts in that church," she began. "My back was *icy*. I knew I was in for it. Odd how it comes so suddenly. And I shake it off suddenly, too." Tom smiled at Marion.

"Most anti-social of me, I know," Margaret went on. "Casting germs in all directions. As soon as I've had this drink, I'll remove myself and take my temperature to bed."

As she passed Tom's chair, she said in a lower voice partially muffled by handkerchief: "That Mrs Veal was at the church." He looked at her and waited, as if what she had said was not enough. "I cut her," she added.

"What an odd thing to have done," he said evenly, watching her go, seeming sunk in his chair, his coat still lapped round him as if he were an old man, refusing to stir.

Marion stood by the window with an empty cup in his hand. Cassandra went out as soon as she thought Margaret had been given time to get into her bedroom. When she reached her own room, she began to pack her small case. The old trunk was filled and strapped down. Now she gathered up the photographs and brushes from the dressing-table. *The Classical Tradition*, she thought, taking the little book from a drawer. What in heaven's name was it all about? She had never read it, and Mrs Turner would expect her to have done so. She put it into the case and unhooked her coat from the great wardrobe where one or two peacock-butterflies hung with wings folded in a winter sleep.

Soon she was ready. She had only her letter to compose. She put her coat on and took her writing things to the window-seat. In the yellowing rose-garden the goose wandered, sedate and forlorn. She dipped her pen into the ink and was about to write when she realised that she had no way of addressing Marion. She had never used his Christian name and could not now. She looked out at the garden, remembering his kiss and its promise of tenderness and intimacy, then dipping the pen in the ink once more wrote very slowly 'Dear Mr Vanbrugh . . .'

CHAPTER FIFTEEN

" I LIKE a nice Sunday film myself," said Nanny, " but as things are I couldn't go."

" Technicolor," said Mrs Adams, peeling potatoes at the sink.

" I can never settle down to technicolor. Some of those blue skies are cruel. An artist wouldn't paint pictures like that. If he did he'd be disqualified."

" It gives more idea of the dresses."

" That I'll grant you. Most of those potatoes seem to be going into the chickens' food. It reminds me of Mrs Courage and the way she used to go into the kitchen every morning to have a look round. ' These potato-peelings! ' she used to say to the kitchen-maid, ' I shall want to see them thinner to-morrow.' It was as much as the girl's position was worth to throw away any of the trimmings and peelings before they were inspected. Not that I'm saying Madam was right going over Cook's head in that way, and in the end Cook left, but she'd have had a word to say about that lot there."

Mrs Adams resented being likened to a kitchen-maid. She was a married woman and not in service. Besides, she was sick and tired of hearing about Mrs Courage, a woman who was not even titled, or only an Honourable, which was no use in conversation.

Nanny straightened things on the dresser, re-arranged the cups so that they all faced the same way and counted the pile of coppers on the shelf.

" All serene," she announced.

" It looks rather pointed it stopping as soon as she leaves. What did he say? "

155

"He shields her. If she took anything worth while with her when she went he'd not let on. After the way he laughed at me I'll never mention it again. I was waiting for *him* to ask about that cameo-brooch. If he'd of said anything to me, 'Well, sir!' I'd have answered, 'I saw it plain as daylight on her dressing-table, but I didn't care to broach the matter, not after the attitude you took up before.'" She savoured the grandeur of this speech for a moment and then went on : "Of course, I didn't know she was going to hop it like she did. He said she was upset. Upset! Much she ever cared for that poor child. If she could leave her on my hands, that suited her. I suppose he posted her money on." ('He's daft enough for anything,' she added to herself.)

"For people in their position it was a poor funeral," said Mrs Adams.

"All the colours of the rainbow," Nanny agreed.

"Not many wreaths."

"If you choose to cut yourself off from society it's not much use expecting a lot of flowers at your funeral."

"Although I say it as shouldn't, Fred was dressed as well as any. He had that suit when he was one of the bearers when the old lady died. He said she was that soaked with port she was as heavy as the spongecake at the bottom of a trifle."

"Perhaps you'll be good enough to get the hall swept," said Nanny. The trouble with Mrs Adams was the old trouble of her taking a yard when she was given only an inch. With the slightest encouragement she became vulgar and had used, on more than one occasion, some very terrible words.

"I'll just run me hands under the tap and put the chickens' food on the boil."

In the hall Tinty was standing on an oak settle underneath which sat the kitchen cat with one paw on a live but paralysed mouse.

156

"A woman's fear of these little creatures has a strange origin," said Margaret coming downstairs and, taking the mouse from the cat's jaws, threw it out of the front door, showing herself to be either less or more than other women. The cat rolled light-heartedly on its back as if freed from a boring duty.

Tinty climbed down shamefacedly as her daughter had intended.

While she was deprecating her cowardice, Mrs Adams came in and began to wrench rugs from under the legs of furniture and throw them on to the terrace outside. Dust rose in clouds and settled in the carved oak.

Margaret had shaken off her 'flu'. She always 'shook off' indispositions, as if the very fact of the illness departing was a sign of her superiority, as perhaps it was.

"Surely you are not going out!" cried Tinty.

"Indeed I am. Two days indoors is more than enough for me."

"I wish you wouldn't. Where *is* everybody?"

"Everybody? There are only Tom and Marion left."

"Please, dear! I *meant* where are *they*? Where is Tom? Where is Marion?"

"What do you want them for?"

"I don't *want* them. I only want to know where they *are*."

"Mother, this seems to be a time, you know, for something to be done about Tom."

Tinty waved her hand and frowned to indicate Mrs Adams coming in with some damp sawdust, which she flung out like chicken-food over the stone floor to settle the dust, by this time mostly lying safe on cornices and banisters and picture frames.

"Because he hasn't deviated for just over a week," Margaret continued as if Mrs Adams were half-witted.

157

"I wish you wouldn't go out, dear, in such doubtful weather."

"I see nothing wrong with the weather," Margaret said, standing at the front door and looking out at the lawns covered with tan-coloured leaves. She was really rather repelled by the look of outdoors, but stepped resolutely over the heap of rugs and went down the steps. Now each leaf at the beginning of its decay was different and interesting. They lay over the drive like shells, like coins, lemon-yellow and black-spotted, or whole fans of chestnut outlined with gold. However much she tried to walk in the middle of the lane, her instinct kept leading her into the ditch, where she shuffled along ankle-deep in beech leaves. The willow trees were hung with strips of grey silk. She leant against the gate half-way down the hill and watched a plough draw one straight furrow across a field. Feeling a little breathless and shivery, she set off again, walking briskly. It would not do for her mother to have been right.

Rain fell softly against her face and then less softly, then like bullets, so hard that she was forced to keep her eyelids lowered. There was nowhere to shelter except the porch of the pub and she ran towards it and stood there very still while the water dripped from her. It was only a shower and already the sky had cleared beyond the park, which was a good thing, for she felt uneasy standing where she was, even so quietly, even so unobserved.

"How do you do," said Mrs Veal, opening the door. "The wretched bell scarcely ever works. Only the merest chance I happened to see you from the saloon bar window. Do come in. How wet you are!"

She had had time to slip on some court shoes and tidy her hair, whereas Margaret was wet and battered and, for the moment, speechless. Mentally she rejected one explanation after another and finally, wiping her shoes on the mat and looking up with a rueful, frank smile, began : " I couldn't go on any longer without apologising, explaining about the other afternoon."

" The other afternoon? " Mrs Veal echoed with feeble incredulity. She led the way into the room with all the ruched cushions and china rabbits. The fire burnt nicely and Gilbert was lying down upstairs.

" At the funeral," Margaret went on, and it was wonderful to hear the confidence gathering again in her voice. " I know I looked right through you, and I should not have waited so long with this apology, but I have had ' flu '."

" Then you shouldn't be out now," said Mrs Veal, thinking of herself.

" Oh, I am not in the least infectious now," Margaret assured her, reading her like a book.

" As if I was thinking of that ! " Mrs Veal made a gesture of dismissal.

" The truth is," Margaret continued, " it was all too much for me. I had to leave the others and go and sit in the car. Perhaps it was the ' flu ' coming on, perhaps not. It has all been rather—much, you know. I thought I was tough, but these days . . . ! " She shrugged and smiled, making a screen of her pregnancy as she had scorned to do before. ' However do I come to be sitting here ? ' she thought, refusing a cigarette, assuring her hostess that a little smoke would not in the least upset her. Mrs Veal was triumphant, like a spider with a live fly in its web. " I just knew that if I spoke to anyone I should . . ." Margaret was saying.

' Is she wearing Tom's shoes ? ' Mrs Veal asked herself. " Of course I understand," she said aloud. " No one feels themselves at a funeral. That poor kiddie. I'm sure I was beyond noticing anything myself." ' She knows I *know* she was sheltering from the rain,' she thought. Yet she respected, as Tom or Marion would not have done, Margaret's dissembling, and even admired her inventiveness and presence of mind. Meanwhile, she had been offering a cup of tea and Margaret had accepted.

There was a creaking sound, a groan, as Gilbert turned over in bed upstairs. 'I'm damned if I'll feed his turkeys, even if he lies there till its dark,' his wife was thinking. " How's your brother? " she asked Margaret casually. " We haven't seen him since that terrible day."

" I don't think you *will* see him again," Margaret said slowly, holding her cup and saucer high above her large stomach.

" Is he going away? "

Margaret heard the danger in that voice, so silken, so tranquil.

" Yes, I think he will go away. My mother and I have worried about him these last few months, but everything seems better lately. We should not like to talk about it to anyone outside the family, but if you understand you might help. He has to be helped, you know, not hindered."

" Do you suggest that I have hindered him? " (The spider was in fact turning into the fly.)

" Only inadvertently. I think you have sometimes made it possible for him to drink more than he should. He has weaknesses, you know . . ."

" I'll say he has weaknesses! " Her hand shook, so she put her cigarette on the fire. " One of his nasty little weaknesses is helping himself to any money that happens to be lying about."

With that sentence she threw up hope, she threw away her last illusions about Tom, all the self-deceptions with which she had helped herself through the last few weeks, her scheming, her dissembling, her hard, hard struggle against her years, and was left empty, not frightened, only spiteful. 'They say nothing can take away your memories,' she thought.

'But bitterness changes them all, makes something else of them. So that once you've felt bitter you've lost the lot.'

One side of Margaret's neck reddened. She recalled Marion telling her to go down to the village to plead for her brother's honour, mocking her. " I wish you would explain," she said wretchedly.

Mrs Veal felt tired. " It was nothing. He couldn't help it."

" You see, it *will* be best if he will go away. Won't you help about it? "

" Nothing I say can make any difference. But he'll go. You needn't worry. There's nothing to keep him here any longer."

Margaret tried to fit a name into this piece of jig-saw. " Cassandra? " she wondered aloud.

"Not her. It isn't in him to care about women any more."

" Then . . . ? "

" Sophy," she said. " While she was alive he would never have left her."

Margaret reddened again at the preposterous insinuation and then whitened because the suggestion was not preposterous at all: it was the missing piece of the puzzle. Everything fell into place and, linking up, had meaning. It was only odd that she had never thought of it before.

" I think I *should* like a cigarette."

Mrs Veal handed her the box, clicked open the lighter. She was a little frightened of what she had done, although her manner was smooth.

"I would never have said anything before. For Sophy's sake."

" Surely she has a sake now she is dead, just as when she was alive? "

" Oh, no! " said Mrs Veal, speaking the truth.

161

" Do people know about this? "

" No. It's all right," she said, her temper whipped up. " You needn't fret, I shall say nothing."

" Of course. I know that," said Margaret, who felt she knew nothing of the kind. " What made you tell me? "

" I don't know." Indeed, she could imagine herself lying awake, night after night, wondering just that.

Upstairs there were creaking sounds all over the floor. Gilbert was up and padding about in his stockinged feet. Mrs Veal wanted Margaret out of the house before he came down, and Margaret wanted to go.

The rain had stopped and the countryside grew still as if settling to a dry, dark evening. Margaret had time to say " thank you " for her tea and be out of the house before Gilbert came down. " You won't . . . ? " Mrs Veal began, as she was closing the door, but after all she closed the door, for now she had dropped the stone into the water and nothing could stop the ripples spreading if they would.

.   .   .   .   .

When Margaret entered the darkening house tea was over and her brother pacing up and down the library, wearing his overcoat.

" In your usual forthright and open-handed way, you have passed on your ' flu ' to me," he complained and tried to cover his face with a large, torn handkerchief before he sneezed.

" I expect it is just a cold, if you are sneezing like that already."

" The name you choose for it makes no odds. The trouble is that I haven't this knack of yours for shaking things off. It will go on for weeks and lower me."

" Tom, when I go back to London, will you come with me? "

She perched on the corner of the table and waited.

He stopped his pacing and leant against a shelf of books.

"With *you*?"

"Yes."

"Good Lord, no! Are you demented?"

She began to explain, rather indistinctly, her head down.

"What did you say?"

"I said that to come with me would make an excuse for doing what you will have to do sooner or later."

"Explain," he said patiently, taking a book from a shelf and seeming to weigh it in his hand.

"Soon Marion is going to know that Sophy was not his child."

"Are you going to enjoy telling him that?"

"You have a poor idea of me," she suggested.

He merely waited.

"I have teased Marion often enough in the past," she went on. "I hope I have never been wantonly cruel. When I look back now it seems that I must often have said things in my ignorance which seemed ironical to you and in the worst taste. But I would not wittingly do anything vicious."

"I always believed that even you would draw the line at some things. I am glad I had so much faith in you and that it has been justified. But if not you, who?"

"Mrs Veal."

"She has a name to you at last, then? Before this she was always 'that woman'. One moment you are cutting her dead in the churchyard, the next moment hatching cosy little plots together."

"I explained that to her."

"It would take some explaining, too, I should think. Even for you."

"Don't keep saying 'even you'. as if I were the dregs of society."

163

"So you think Marion is going to throw me out, or horse-whip me down the drive? But you have overlooked what is called a salient point . . . or perhaps it would be better to say the crux of the matter—both expressions delight me so, I don't know which to choose. . . ."

"You are trying to make me impatient."

"The crux of the matter is . . ." he replaced the book . . . "that Marion knows already."

Margaret looked angry. "How could he? And *you*? How could you stay here? How long has he known?"

"He knew—let me see——" Tom considered . . . "I should say about nine months before Sophy was born."

Margaret burst into tears at the shock. Perhaps it was a good thing that Tinty had an instinct for arriving at such times.

"Tom! Margaret darling! I've been watching from the window for you. How can I have missed you? Tom, what-ever you have been saying to upset your sister, it is really too thoughtless of you. You know how lowering ' flu ' is."

"I shall soon find out."

"This cold library, too! I lit a fire in the drawing-room. Let's all settle down and have a nice cosy evening together. We so seldom do. Cheer up, darling. I will make you a cup of tea, and there is a lovely surprise for you on the mantel-piece in the drawing-room. A large fat letter from Ben."

"From large fat Ben," said Tom.

Tinty looked warningly at him, as she used to look when he was a child and showed off in company.

"It came by the afternoon post, soon after you had gone out," she went on, coaxing Margaret towards the drawing-room.

As soon as they had gone, Tom went quickly towards Marion's room, taking the stairs two at a time. Marion was sitting at the table writing a letter.

"Margaret is crying," Tom said at once.

"How awkward."

"She is crying because of a lie I told her." He went to the fire, putting himself at Marion's back.

"You had better go and untell it then, and perhaps she will stop."

"It doesn't in the least matter if she stops or not. But I came to turn the lie into the truth."

"What is all this?" But Marion went on writing, not concerned. He felt that nothing would concern him much again.

"I don't know how men say these sorts of things to one another," Tom said, looking at Marion's back in the mirror. "I am not callous, but I find I can only say it as it is—that Sophy was not your child, but mine."

Marion made a full stop and then turned it into a comma and waited.

"Don't let it change Sophy for you. Children are people. Not bits of grown-ups." He kicked at a log on the fire and flames crackled up round his shoe. "Margaret taxed me with it just now. It cannot be denied. I've always realised that. As soon as people begin to look into the matter, it's all up."

"Are they beginning to look into it?" Marion asked coldly.

"Margaret was. I told her you had always known. That was the famous lie."

"Thank you."

"I'm sorry."

"No, I *meant* thank you. In an obscure way it seems to save some of my pride. What put the idea into Margaret's head?"

"She seems to have been hobnobbing (that seems to be exactly the word for it) with a friend of mine at the pub—

a Mrs Veal, a rather tough and tawdry person I am closely, nay intimately, acquainted with."

Marion laid down his pen and at last turned round in his chair to look at Tom. In a different voice he asked : " This is absolutely true, Tom? Beyond all doubt?"

Tom nodded. " You shouldn't have married her," he said loudly. " She was always mine."

" I didn't force her, or carry her off."

" You used her weakness and her impatience. You had money : I had none. She would have had to wait years for me, and waiting for anything unnerved her so that she no longer wanted it. Then *you* believed her to be good. I knew her to be bad and sometimes she hated me for knowing it."

" I don't know what you mean by all this ' good ' and ' bad '. Nor all this about money. She was a person of spirit and intelligence, not someone out of a comic song, not this bird in a gilded cage you describe."

" If she were going out to tea, I had only to look at her across the table at lunch to throw her into a state of panic and indecision.

" Oh, damn you! Damn you! "

Marion walked up and down and with each step he encountered a revelation he could not endure.

" How long after we were married? Oh, not long, of course," he said quickly to cover the wound and avoid seeming too pathetic.

" It had never stopped," Tom said, to blot out from Marion's mind any crude idea of his own inadequacy. " Not since she was eighteen."

" Oh, my God! Why did you let me do this to you both? "

" *She* did it. She turned me into a sort of glowering Heathcliff. But she *was* punished. A great deal. More than she deserved."

" Tom, we are grown-up people. I don't understand this

166

in you—this talk of good and bad and deserving punishment. What next? The coils of fate?"

"No, not that far." Tom smiled. "You see, I am speaking all the old thoughts that used to come from my conscience when I was very young, and good and bad had separate meanings."

"What does Margaret intend to do?"

"Nothing, I expect. She likes to irritate, not devastate people."

"It is odd that you could have told Mrs Veal."

"I didn't. Don't look at me like that. The woman has no sensibility, but she seems to have perception. She cottons-on to things. Her fiendish jealousy makes her 'intuitive'."

"Did you guess she had—cottoned-on to this?"

"No. No, but I think I felt her vaguely threatening."

"What will *she* do?"

"I will see that she does nothing." When he had said this he sat down, feeling full of tired horror.

"Don't take her life," Marion sneered. "We shall have had our fill of gossip and melodrama."

"There is an easier way than that of keeping her quiet." 'But it goes on longer,' he thought, resting his forehead against the palms of his hands.

"Please make no sacrifice on my account."

Marion sat down again at the table and picked up the pen.

"Who are you writing to?"

"I am trying to write to Cassandra. I thought of asking her to marry me. So if you and she have any little secrets, it would be doing me a favour if you would tell me now. Or forever hold your peace."

"Don't write to her. Go to her!"

"I know you are always successful with women, but I didn't ask your advice."

167

While Marion wrote, Tom sat huddled up in his overcoat by the fire. Presently he got up and went towards the door.

" Tom ! "

" Yes."

They looked at one another awkwardly.

" I'm sorry, Tom. I feel so damned foolish."

" I know."

" *You* are still the same person to me."

He noted the inflexion, but said nothing.

" Just now, I was trying to work myself into a rage against you, into seeing you as someone different, but I couldn't."

" Do we shake hands now, do you think ? " Tom inquired.

Marion laughed and then, his glance skidding away, said : " Only one thing . . . you must be truthful about it . . . you and Violet . . . I suppose you thought me pathetic and absurd . . . did you laugh about me, or hate me . . . ? "

" Nothing. She would never have let you be mentioned," Tom lied. He went out then and shut the door quickly, knowing that only a state of agony could have forced such a question from his cousin.

Marion wrote the address upon the square, white envelope and sat staring at it. After a long while he tore it across and dropped it on the fire.

CHAPTER SIXTEEN

MRS VEAL, who had given up hope of Tom, was dishevelled when he walked in. She came closer to the bar, wishing to hide the old evening shoes she was wearing. He knew that she would say 'Hullo, stranger!' She did so.

He sat down on the stool in the corner and looked at her without answering.

She thought: 'All the time he was bound to come back. Why didn't I know?'

It was soon after opening-time and he was the first customer. Only Gilbert was walking in and out in his shirt-sleeves, carrying crates.

"What are you having?"

"Scotch." He laid down a note.

She leant her elbow on the bar and watched him drinking, and when Gilbert had gone out for a moment she said in a low voice: "I wanted to say how sorry I was about . . . I felt so much for you, but I . . ."

Tom ignored her. Gilbert walked in.

"How's his lordship?" she asked in a different voice.

"He has gone away," Tom said, knowing she meant Marion. He felt angry with his cousin. 'It is on account of him that I am here,' he explained to himself. 'If it were just me to be considered, I should never darken the threshold of this place again. Although it could not easily be darker than it is.'

"Yes," he said carelessly. "He has gone after the governess and I think he will ask her to marry him."

"What if she refuses?" Mrs Veal asked, not able to believe in Marion's success.

"She won't. It is never done."

Gilbert took his place behind the bar and poured the first light ale of the evening for Charlie, who came in smoking a cigar.

"Good God. What's this? Old rope?" asked Gilbert.

"That's right. Try one." Charlie took another from his waistcoat pocket and Gilbert held it to his ear, sniffed at it and then put it up on a shelf until he could sell it later to someone else.

"I'll have it when I've got me strength up. Can't have two of us turning away good custom."

"That's right." Charlie drew at the cigar, savouring it, holding it out at arm's length. "I'd like to see them native girls rolling them on their bare thighs."

"Go on," said Mrs Veal, turning to him.

"God's truth."

"Black girls?"

She wrinkled her nose.

"Well, coffee-coloured. Better still. What say you, Gilbert?"

"Suits me," he said absent-mindedly, bringing in a handful of filled tankards, setting them down before another of the Boys, who said at once: "What's old Charlie got hold of? Burning the hair off his chest?"

"Don't be disgusting," said Mrs Veal.

"I don't think you quite understood what I said." He winked at her as he drank. "Do Corona to-day, Gil?"

"I certainly did. *Very* nice."

Tom rolled a half-crown along the bar towards Mrs Veal, then slammed his hand flat over it. She took his glass and filled it. Under cover of the other's talk, he said (insulting in that playful way to which no one is supposed to take exception): "By the way, I am bloody angry with you."

"What have I done, pray?" she asked, perching herself

on the high stool behind the bar, shrugging her shoulders. She tried to be cool, but was only arch.

"You see," Gilbert was saying loudly as a customer went out. "Just one quick drink and good night for everyone this evening." He looked at Charlie's cigar.

"No wonder," said Mrs Veal, turning deliberately away from Tom towards Charlie and fanning the blue smoke with her hand.

"If you weren't sitting on it I'd slap your wrist."

"That's enough of that sort of talk," she said daintily.

"Drink up then and forgive. What is it? Guinness?"

Tom never bought her a drink, and she accepted Charlie's in such a way, she hoped, as to underline Tom's meanness. She put her lip into the brown froth and then dabbed at her mouth with a lace handkerchief. Presently, against her will, her eyes came back to Tom.

"Please don't," she said suddenly in a low voice.

"I hadn't realised you wanted to drive me away," he said, knowing he sounded childish. "That is the effect you are having. Your imagination is a little too much of a good thing. You tell your lies by implication, which is always the most efficient way." He looked round the bar casually as he spoke.

"*Have* I told a lie?"

"Yes, but unfortunately it is a lie against which the truth would shrivel away. It would be too delightful. People "— he glanced round the bar—" would find it irresistible."

"How would people ever come to hear of it?" She glanced round too.

He waited for her to finish her Guinness, then he said: "If people do not come to hear of it there is no more to be said."

Charlie's cigar was the joke of the evening, but it could not last for ever. There was even a little horse-play of the kind which Gilbert permitted his regular customers, but when

Tom laid down the money for another whisky he lowered his eyelids at his wife, which was his way of warning her against encouraging drunkenness. She pretended not to see.

"And a Guinness," said Tom suddenly, adding more money to his change and pushing it towards her.

"Cheers then." She lifted the glass. They seemed cut off from the others.

"Good luck."

And so they made their bargain, without putting it into too many words: as people do make bargains when ashamed of the sound of the words.

.　　　.　　　.　　　.　　　.

The light was enough to read by. The moon, an uncertain shape, like a broken plate, set this incandescent radiance over the house and garden; fell, not impartially, as rain does, but capriciously, it seemed, striking one chimney-pot but not the next, leaving the steps in blackness, yet revealing a single ivy-leaf silvered by a snail in the shrubbery.

The walls of the house were whitened, leprous, and even the moon which illuminated them had a scarred look as if pitted by disease.

Tom's feet seemed to strike the ground at different levels, coming up the drive, changing from one course to another, the laurels brushing his shoulders as he strayed from side to side.

The moonlight was pearly, very muted and dusty over the wreckage of the conservatory. When Tom came to it he found he could not indulge in his familiar, transitory annoyance with Marion. Like a cataract gathering speed, the sheets of cracked and splintered glass had come down a night or two ago, started by some small thing, something never to be known, a twig falling, an owl flying, or merely the last imperceptible change of quantity, a foreshadowing of what might happen to the house itself, how, after a long process of decay, one day it would suddenly not be a house any more.

Tom looked at the ragged palm-leaves which were dipped in silver and the little flags and pennants of glass still left on pieces of the shattered framework. He felt that all of the past was quite broken now, his fears broken last of all. Violet gone. Sophy gone. Marion gone. And the moonlight fell with malice upon his tears. 'A crying jag now,' he thought, blundering towards the house. Self-pity dragged at him, sucking him down, as waves tug down the shingle on the beach into oblivion. Going upstairs he clung to the thought of Marion and went unsteadily along the passage, burst open the door ready to dramatise himself and unburden himself as he had done countless times before. But the door opened upon darkness.

Like a child he began to cry, one hand over his face, the other fumbling along the walls for the light-switch. The room was cold and tidy, with no fire, no coffee-pot, the books stacked neatly and the cushions uncreased. When he remembered that Marion was away and remembered why, he could not believe in his bad luck. Despair took him right down. He touched the bottom of the sea. Aimlessly, he went round the room. He picked up Violet's and Cassandra's Greek books, opened and interlocked, he caught a glimpse of his stained, tired eyes in a mirror, he opened a drawer in a little table by the fireplace and took out a cameo-brooch. He carried it in his hand to the light and sat down at the big table in the middle of the room, remembering some fuss, some quarrel about this brooch and puzzling over it. Ideas seemed to come first from one side of his head, then the other, they mingled and dissolved. In this way, wearing his overcoat, with the brooch lying in his open hand, he fell asleep, his head dropping on his crooked arm, in Violet's room.

173

CHAPTER SEVENTEEN

"No, dear, I don't exactly think you did wrong. I merely said I thought you didn't do right . . . I only mean that it is a little awkward. . . ." 'Awkward' was a favourite word with Mrs Turner. She rarely allowed herself a stronger expression.

"One can hardly go on being a governess to a dead child."

Although Mrs Turner was not used to rudeness, she detected the glitter of tears behind Cassandra's stubborn glance.

"But, dear, a little talk with Mr Vanbrugh would have settled things more pleasantly."

"We had nothing to say to one another."

"That was for him to decide. He was your employer, and later there will be a question of references." ('And your money,' she thought.)

'One doesn't ask for references from those one loves,' Cassandra thought. What, for instance, could he write about her—"During the few months Miss Dashwood was in my employ, she proved herself to be honest and reliable."

"It was quite the last thing I would have wished for you, dear. The very worst thing, when you so needed taking out of yourself. You will look back upon this year as one when all your troubles came at once. I daresay most people have such years, but you are very young to be so disheartened. All the same, I wish you had not run away. There was no . . . nothing unpleasant . . ." her voice wavered uncertainly.

"What *can* be more unpleasant than what happened?" On the morning of the funeral she had picked up from a flower-bed under the terrace a bunch of stone grapes freckled

with blood and had carried it in her hand and thrown it into
the shrubbery so that Marion might never find it.

"I should write a letter to Mr Vanbrugh," Mrs Turner
suggested.

"I did write him one."

"And he hasn't replied?"

"No."

"Come in!" Mrs Turner called out, and a girl with her
hair in elaborate fronds about her forehead looked in.

"Oh, Alma. I will see you in one moment."

The door shut again.

"I must have a little talk with Alma. She has seemed to
be kicking against the pricks this term, I thought. Her essay
last week on 'The Road to Damascus' was so . . . she seems
a little to have lost her balance . . . and then this silly business
about the nail-varnish . . . it is difficult to know the best
attitude to adopt . . . they are all trivial symptoms, I know;
but symptoms none the less, and I thought a little talk . . .
Anyhow, Cassandra, I shall shoo you away now . . . think
over what I have said . . . although indeed I seem to have
said nothing. . . . If I were you I'd take a walk before . . .
unless Mademoiselle wants any help with the little ones . . .
If you are passing Tucker's here is this book-list to be left . . .
and will you ask Alma to come in, dear . . ."

Alma stood in the hall, fiddling with her hair and using
a large picture of the Giant's Causeway as a mirror. She
pulled up her stockings and entered Mrs Turner's room, and
Cassandra heard Mrs Turner's voice, so hopeful so encouraging, beginning: "Now, Alma . . ." as the door was
shut.

Cassandra went out through the cloakroom, which really
was a cloakroom, to the leaf-cluttered drive. The sun after a
brilliant autumn day suddenly clouded, leaving the sky, the
landscape enclosed in blue. Girls walked back across the

playing-fields wearing green and red girdles. Once, out there, Cassandra, standing at the edge of the circle for a penalty corner, had had the ball rebound from her stick into the goal. Little girls had capered at the touch-line, mistresses had clapped their fur-backed gloves together and she had walked to the centre feeling a hypocrite for the first time in her life.

Upstairs, in the music-room, a girl scrooped on a violin. At moments the melody rang out clearly and purely as if it were the untouched vision of the adolescent, and then faltered, for there was no more to it than the adolescent's lack of skill and the choked emotions which had neither coherence nor direction. "The Snowy-Breasted Pearl".

As she began to walk downhill away from the school she could hear the trams going by on the main road and the sound evoked the empty past and seemed to promise that the future should be no different.

She walked past her old home. The brick front was covered with the reddish stalks of virginia-creeper; a plant with oiled leaves stood in a bronze pot between folk-weave curtains; a pram blocked the doorway. Ivy's baby? Across the road lights glittered in the little shops.

She went on towards Tucker's, for Mrs Turner's so carelessly thrown-out suggestions were in reality commands, as all her pupils were aware. Tucker's was another detail of the past which had continued, it seemed, just as if she had never gone away and which, so unaltered, made no sign of recognition now that she had returned, even displayed the same title-pages in the windows, the same wretched dregs in the threepenny box by the door. Once, coming out of that door, reading a copy of *The Picture of Dorian Gray* which she had just bought for ninepence, Cassandra had met Mrs Turner, who had told her to close her book at once and look where she was going. "Life is short, but not so short that

176

we must go about the streets reading, spoiling our eyes and running under tramcars and looking studious . . ."

She handed in the list at the counter and went through to the back of the shop, where shelves dipped in the middle under the weight of tightly-wedged volumes. The books walled her in impersonally, so that she could be alone with herself as if she were in church or in a thick wood.

Now she was parted from Marion, she had over-reached her loving and arrived at the state of infatuation in which to read his name in print in a telephone directory, or the name of his house upon a map, filled her with a cherished melancholy, her eyes loving each letter of his name and seeing upon the map so many things no other eyes would have seen. She took down one Greek book after another, tormenting herself, then a book on architecture with prints of houses, some a little like his, some quite unlike, even opened a copy of *The Provoked Wife*, for at least the surname on the title-page was the same, the letters of the alphabet arranged in that right miraculous order.

"You are not trying to improve yourself," said Marion, his shadow falling suddenly over the page.

It was intolerable to him to see her so overcome, even he, who had never, it had lately appeared, been loved until now, and had wished to be.

"Mrs Turner sent me to find you. It was no coincidence."

"Why did you come?"

"I will tell you that when we are outside."

Taking the book from her hands, he carried it to the counter and paid for it and then, with her elbow in his hand, brought her out—as if she were a sleep-walker, or blind—into the quiet iris-coloured dusk and along the pavement.

"I am staying here to-night," he said, suddenly stopping by an hotel with a large stuffed bear holding a lantern above the porch. "I told Mrs Turner I would give you some tea.

177

She seemed very worried about you having a cup of tea and I must keep my promise."

The vestibule was covered with drugget and very hushed. A porter spoke in whispers to a waiter. The walls were correctly hung with " The Rake's Progress ", in keeping with the gentility of the place.

The lounge was empty. As they entered, the last remnants of pale coal shuddered together in the grate.

' If he asks me why I ran away, what in heaven's name can I say ? ' Cassandra wondered, sitting down on a window-seat where a draught lifted the cretonne curtains. Marion, looking more austere than ever in these surroundings, gave orders about buttered toast and tea.

With her worn glove twisted round the handle of the teapot, she poured two wavering streams of tea into the cups.

"I worried about you," he said, watching her, feeling that she had become strangely dear to him. "And not just about cups of tea and if you are getting them, but about you yourself, and whether you were happy or unhappy."

She ate a strip of toast without tasting it.

" I tried one letter after another and none of them would do. So I came myself."

" I can't eat any more," she said, shaking her head at the plate offered.

" The fact is, Tom told me to come. It was his idea."

" How is Tom ? " she asked, not caring.

Marion took a piece of toast and looked at it. " ' Let the world slide. Have not you maggots in your brain.' I mean Tom, my dear," for Cassandra looked surprised. " There's another thing about Tom . . . if you have ever been in a tent in the pouring rain . . . You know how threatening it seems, with the canvas so drenched and taut and swollen, but you are sure of being safe unless you touch it. Tom could never

178

bear not to after a time, and now he is drowning." This metaphor, like the quotation, pleased him, because it meant nothing and betrayed nobody.

"And Margaret?" she asked, lifting the lid of the hot water jug and peeping inside.

"Margaret is as much the same as she can be expected to be. In fact, more so. Her child is as long being born as Tristram Shandy. I can never turn an expectant mother out into the falling leaves, but neither can I much longer bear to have her in the house. I thought those things could always be counted on to take no longer than nine months. That consoled me and kept me going, but nature is not to be relied upon, it seems."

"Perhaps it is long to her, too."

"Ah, you see, you are on her side. When you went away, you left the cameo-brooch I gave you. Why?" He looked at her throat where it should have been.

"Taking it was—not a thing I could do."

"Margaret brought your letter to me that evening. I shall never forget her standing in the doorway with the brooch in one hand and the letter in the other, as if it were the dénouement."

Cassandra flushed, for her action appeared melodramatic now and she saw that it must have seemed so to him.

"What have you been doing?" he asked.

"Helping in the kindergarten. Running errands for Mrs Turner."

"Mrs Turner was being very grave with a frightening sort of a girl who kept shaking her hair back off her shoulders. Although the child sat and made eyes at me, her handkerchief was rolled into a damp little ball in her hands."

"She has been writing some very awkward little essays," said Cassandra. "One about Saint Francis and the Stigmata, which Mrs Turner thought hysterical and unnecessary. And

179

she has been varnishing her nails—only pink varnish, of course."

"Pink nails are the worst. They look like cheap sweets, I think. She doesn't know whether to be a nymphomaniac or a religious maniac. In another year, there will be no doubt at all."

As she took a cigarette from him her fingers trembled.

"Cassandra, dear, I don't really want to sit here talking about schoolgirls, but it seems such an odd and awful place to be asking you to marry me." ('Tom would not have let it happen like this,' he thought.) "Will you? I imagined that after that night when there was the thunderstorm that you would understand that I love you. Yet, when I thought about it, it seemed that all I had to give you was stale and complicated, that you were too young to be drawn into my life, and that disheartening house, so ramshackle and remote —the other night the conservatory fell in. Tom always said it would——" He pushed his empty cup away from him as if it were something more distasteful to him than a cup could be—"and then Aunt Tinty—I am like a wreck with barnacles clinging to me—she is so ineffectual, so exasperating, and Nanny so old and venomous. I am quite encumbered by them." He said nothing about Tom.

'They can't live for ever,' Cassandra thought placidly, with the calm optimism of youth.

"And then, into the middle of my mind-searchings and before I could talk to you, it happened about Sophy and nothing could be said."

'The chief obstacle he hides,' Cassandra thought, seeing the ghost of Violet, palely coloured like her name. 'That is the only real obstacle between us, the only one which will be there for ever and ever, and scares me and threatens me— his memories of her perfection, in the light of which I shall always fail.'

'I ought to kiss her,' he thought wretchedly, glancing quickly round the lounge. He did not want to take her hand under cover of the tablecloth and said suddenly: "Shall we go? Although I have no idea where to." He wondered where Tom would have taken her—to the cinema, to a corner of some noisy pub?

"I shall have to go back. There are jobs I have to do at the children's bedtime."

He remembered Sophy standing by the window in her dressing-gown, while Cassandra plaited her hair.

They went along the drugget to the swing-doors. The street lights were shaggy and blurred chrysanthemums in the misty air. Windows blossomed high upon buildings.

"This house is where I used to live," Cassandra said, stopping for a moment at the corner to look at the light shed through the honey-coloured blind at an upstairs window and a shadow crossing and recrossing what had been her bedroom once. She felt a great strangeness that she should be standing there with Marion, looking up at the house from outside, and the trams and traffic going down the dip of the road under the railway arch, sounding so different now, for they emphasised how changed her life was to be.

The front door opened and a fan of light and voices came out of the hall. Marion and Cassandra moved on, turning from the main road and climbing up the quiet hill towards the school, between the blank darkness of the houses, where lamplight fell upon the branches of trees with their few leaves. Each time they came to a lamp he looked at her, her paper-white face and dark mouth and her bare head shining. Once he asked: "And you truly love me?"

"Yes."

"Since when?"

The shadow of leaves passed over her face, and then darkness.

"Since the evening when we walked in the park first of all," she said, knowing that it was before that. Before she saw him or spoke to him, she had determined to love him, as if she were a governess in a book. Meeting him had merely confirmed her intention, made possible what she had hoped.

At the school gate, she stopped and put her hand on his arm. "Let me go in alone."

"Your Mrs Turner will think it awkward and boorish of me."

"I shall go straight up to the playroom. I shan't see her until after prayers."

"And you will marry me?"

"Yes."

"Soon? Very soon?"

"Yes, please."

"Dearest Cassandra, I will be very good to you."

"Marion."

"Yes?" She merely felt that the moment of saying it was the happiest of her life.

"Good night."

As she turned away: 'I mustn't say it too often,' she decided, hurrying up the drive.

He walked down the hill and looked again at her house, filled with the tenderest sensations, and then made his way along the road towards the bear with the lantern.

.   .   .   .   .

After prayers Cassandra drank a cup of Benger's with Mrs Turner.

"Did you leave the list at Tucker's dear?"

"Yes, Mrs Turner."

"Oh, your Mr Vanbrugh called and I sent him after you. I hope he found you, but he wouldn't wait and really it was the least bit inconvenient . . . Alma at her worst wanting to take the veil, as she herself puts it. Every five years or so I get a girl who has this unsettling influence. It gives the school a bad tone, and it *is* extraordinary how from one girl at the top it can sift down to the youngest in the kindergarten. I don't want to worry her father . . . he has other problems . . . he's a clergyman and would be upset . . . I tried to keep my manner very dry and brisk . . . 'You would certainly have less trouble about your hair,' I told her, for the subtle ways she has of making herself look sophisticated irritate one very much, I'm afraid. 'Oh, I am willing to sacrifice my hair,' she said and began to cry. Sacrifice her hair, indeed! How she gets such notions is beyond me."

"Mrs Turner, I am going to be married."

"And a very much nicer idea, too, my dear," said Mrs Turner, who had only chattered while she waited for Cassandra to announce this. "I expect it is this Mr Vanbrugh. I knew all along that there was some sort of nonsense going on. Well, we must have a good long talk about it, but not now, for you seem quite fagged. Drink up your Benger's and get an early night."

Cassandra drank and stood up.

"Good night, Mrs Turner."

"Good night, my dear. And I do wish you very, very happy. It is one nice thing there has been to-day. I thought he seemed a very pleasant young man and not at all what I had imagined, although I felt that any cousin of Margaret's *must* be nice."

"Mrs Turner."

"What is it, dear?"

"Have you a copy of *Tristram Shandy*? I have often *meant* to read it and never have."

"Yes, dear, I think you will find it on the top-but-one shelf by the door there. A red book. Rather middle-sized,

183

because it is small print. No, there it is next to *Little Women*. What odd neighbours. It was my husband's."

" May I borrow it? "

" Of course, dear, but don't tire your eyes. Certainly take it if you can make head or tail of it. I never could."

" Good night."

" Good night, dear."

Cassandra sped across the hall and upstairs. And Mrs Turner took a large piece of striped knitting from a bag and put on her spectacles.

.   .   .   .   .

Upstairs, Alma took up her slipper to squash a large spider on the wall above her chest-of-drawers, but remembered in time. Luckily, the girl in the next bed leaned over and smacked at it with her Bible.

.   .   .   .   .

Marion went to bed early, too. As he drew back the sooty curtains and opened the window which faced a wall, he wondered what they were doing at home, remembering how the windows there opened out into the dark tangle of garden, the house creaking, sighing, rustling with mice.

" Perhaps we could get a cook," he was thinking, with the bright optimism of those about to marry.

.   .   .   .   .

" And she is so pale," Mademoiselle marvelled; Mrs Turner was only human and keeping good news to herself emphasised her widowhood unbearably.

" She is very young."

But Mademoiselle considered the paleness, not her youth, Cassandra's great disability. " And it is a very large house? "

184

"One of those country manor houses," said Mrs Turner complacently.

Mademoiselle saw a long, turreted façade, castellated, machicolated, at the end of a poplar-bordered drive.

"A large domestic staff, for sure?"

"One of his aunts is his housekeeper," Mrs Turner hedged.

Mademoiselle imagined nothing at all like Tinty, but a chatelaine in alpaca with keys to stillroom, linen-closet and buttery. "And the little girl has died, God-rest-her-soul?" It was all most satisfactory. "The bridegroom is charming?"

"Well . . ." Mrs Turner's eyes measured the striped knitting. "He was very civil and . . . he is not a very masculine type. By that I mean he looks delicate in a girlish sort of way . . . a studious young man . . ."

"Young?"

"In his mid-thirties, no more. You must remember his cousin, Margaret Vanbrugh?"

"Ah, she was a capable, nice girl."

So Margaret made everything right for Marion, her capability cancelled his effeminacy.

.   .   .   .   .

Cassandra lay in bed reading. Her eyes travelled along the lines of print and then she sighed and turned back to page one again.

CHAPTER EIGHTEEN

THE WEEPING fell to Mrs Turner at the wedding, since
Cassandra had no mother, nothing very much in the way of
female relations. Mrs Turner wept very well, not in a steady
way as at funerals, but in a gusty, fussy, protesting fashion,
dabbing at her eyes and smiling at her own foolishness.
Cassandra very properly looked 'like a snowdrop', was
rather timid and shy, which is better, perhaps, than being
masterful. Marion had neuralgia.

Margaret had stayed at home, unable to travel because
of the uncertainty of " her Dates ". ("Are you sure, darling,
you didn't get your Dates wrong? " her mother asked many
times as the days wore on. " Oh, I know *you* should know
best, dear, but it *is* a little . . . I don't understand these obstet-
rical calendars and all this about *lunar* months. I always
counted up say from the 31st of January . . ." "Always? "
Margaret asked. " It sounds as if you spent your entire life
in child-bed.") So Tinty stayed with her, and the suitcase for
the nursing-home stood ready in the hall.

Tom was best man and was heavily jocular towards
Marion, as if giving him a treat : really, his mind was not
on what he was doing. He flirted a little with the bride, so
that Mademoiselle saw an interesting situation ahead of
Cassandra, and felt embittered when she thought that a
girl, so pale, so poor, with so execrable a French accent,
should fall into this lap of luxury, this vast estate and staff.
And two young men.

Margaret and Tinty, left alone, felt that the fewer people
were in the house, the less it seemed able to support its existence. The sound of voices—of doors slamming—seemed to

have prolonged its life beyond what was natural and to be expected. But as the life was gradually withdrawn, the house became a shell only, seeming to foreshadow its own strange future when leaves would come into the hall, great antlered beetles run across the hearths, the spiders let themselves down from the ceilings to loop great pockets of web across corners; plaster would fall, softly, furtively, like snow, birds nest in the chimneys and fungus branch out in thick layers in the rotting wardrobes. Then the stone floor of the hall would heave up and erupt with dandelion and briar, the bats swing up the stairs and the dusty windows show dark stars of broken glass. As soon as grass grows in the rooms and moles run waveringly down passages, the house is not a house any more, but a monument, to show that in the end man is less durable than the mole and cannot sustain his grandeur.

So, "You would think," said Margaret to her mother, "that he would have run to a coat of paint for his bride. She must love him very much."

"Why should that be surprising?" asked Tinty. "It seems a very proper emotion for a bride to feel."

"I mean, her love will be much put to the test. On the whole, though, decrepit as it all is, I think I was better here than at home in the flat," Margaret said, as if she had conferred a favour upon her cousin. She was beginning to speak of her pregnancy (which still went on) in the past tense. "We shall have to take the napkins and the nightgowns out of the case and air them." She went out and fetched the baby-clothes, hanging them about in front of the fire, where they gently steamed.

"We can't have these lying about in the drawing-room when the bride arrives," said Tinty. "Nanny can hang them on the airer in the kitchen."

"I wonder how Tom behaved at the wedding. He and Marion should be getting into their stride by now, good team-work and so on. Their partnership in all these different ceremonies has given them so much practice. If I have a son" (and she realised that she would), "they shall both be his godfathers. It will be a change for them to be standing at a font."

"I wish you wouldn't talk like that," said her mother, which was a phrase she had been repeating all her life. "I wonder what Nanny is doing?"

"The last time I saw her she was in her chair in the kitchen sticking large black pins into a wax image of Cassandra."

"Don't be silly, dear. There is no need for there to be any trouble, unless you stir it up."

"I suppose she won't live much longer," said Margaret. "It is an odd world where the young die so much and the old live so ruinously long. She will fall asleep in her rocking-chair when she is a hundred-and-something. A nice peaceful death, quite undeserved."

But Nanny was going round the bedrooms, a duster in her hand lest she should be caught prying. She dusted Violet's photograph and drew it a little forward, in front of Sophy's. Marion had thought it would be melodramatic to put his first wife's picture away, although he had no particular wish to look at it ever again. Nanny felt, as politicians say they feel after wars, as if a great new era was opening up before her.

Going along the landing, she avoided Tom's room because Bony gave her the horrors and once she had discovered there a drawing Tom had done of herself in a coffin, wearing a nightgown trimmed with valenciennes lace and an enamelled brooch her mother had given her painted with rosebuds and the name "Frances".

.   .   .   .   .

"I wonder what Cassandra wore at the wedding," Tinty was saying.

"I guess white lace," said Margaret

"Do you remember Violet in the grey velvet? It was really very unsuitable for a wedding, but she did look lovely with the dark red roses."

"I thought she looked demented in that dress," said Margaret, who had been married at Caxton Hall in a fur coat.

"Excuse me, madam," said Nanny, at the door.

Tinty looked round suspiciously.

"I thought, madam, you ought to have out some wine and biscuits for their arrival."

"Oh, that is a very good idea. Why didn't I think of it earlier? I'm sure they would appreciate it."

"There are the little almond biscuits. They are rather soft, so I have crisped them up in the oven."

"How thoughtful of you, Nanny. What do you think about the wine?"

"Madeira would be suitable," said Nanny, who fancied a glass of this. "It's a wine no one could take any exception to a young girl drinking."

When she had shut the door, Margaret said idly: "What did I tell you about the black pins? No one can say I started up that particular bit of bother."

"Here is the car!" cried Tinty, running towards the hall. "Why, she is wearing the very coat she wore the first day she ever came here."

. . . . .

The day after Marion and Cassandra returned, Margaret went to the nursing home to be delivered of a large male child.

After breakfast that morning Tom had said: "Margaret,

how much longer is this to go on? We are at the end of our tether. Besides, Cassandra deserves to be the centre of attention now. You had your turn when you were first married. I thought she looked very pretty at breakfast."

"She has made the change from governess to mistress of the house very charmingly," said Tinty. "It is like one of the fairy tales."

"But not a fairy tale in which I should want to be the heroine," said Margaret. "One begins to see what is meant by 'they lived happily ever after'."

"What are they doing now?" asked Tinty, who always liked to know where people were.

"I think he is giving her a Greek lesson," said Tom.

"No, they have gone to look at the conservatory," said Tinty, leaning out of the window and seeing them together on the drive. "Marion wonders what can be done with it."

"He will never get beyond wondering."

．　　　．　　　．　　　．　　　．

"It came down like an avalanche," Marion was saying. The palm tree stood up among the mountain of dusty, shattered glass, not impressive, only absurd.

It was a cold morning, but sunny, and they took a short walk down the lime avenue. When they came to the animals' graves and the grassy mound, Cassandra said: "What *is* this?"

"It was the old ice house. I had it filled in a long time ago, because it was dangerous to children."

There had never been any children. Only Sophy.

"I shall get all these dead laurels cut out," he went on. "Clear up some of this timber."

Halfway up the avenue he said: "Darling, I thought at breakfast and last night that you managed very sweetly. It isn't fair of me to ask you to put up with all these people, but I admire you for the gentle way you have with them."

" Only Nanny frightens me."

" She can't live for ever."

As they neared the house they found a taxi throbbing at the foot of the steps.

" Is it . . . could it be Margaret at last? " asked Cassandra, and ran up the steps into the house ahead of Marion.

Mrs Adams rushed through the baize door into the hall with a pile of napkins. " The water's broke, miss, I mean Madam."

" What water? " Cassandra asked stupidly.

" Madam's started her pains."

Out on the drive the taxi-driver swung his arms back and forth across his chest and stamped his feet. ' It is not as cold as all that,' Marion thought, coming up the steps into the house.

Margaret came downstairs in her fur coat, her watch in her hand. It was as if she were something they had all awaited. She came slowly down the stairs. Tinty followed. Her face was pale and she had covered it with a blue net veil.

" Are you timing yourself? " Tom enquired, fascinated by the watch. " Good-bye, Margaret, I am sure you will manage very well."

Margaret came to Cassandra and kissed her. To Marion she said: "Thank you, Marion, for putting up with me all this long time."

He could hardly say it had been a pleasure and murmured in his throat instead.

" I want to go before Nanny has time to say I shall be worse before I am better," said Margaret, and went down the steps, refusing her cousin's arm. Tinty followed.

Nanny was with Mrs Adams at a window upstairs. Both

were full of the forebodings of birth, of reminiscence and gloomy prophecy. They saw the cab heave over as Margaret stepped into it, watched the case put in beside the driver and Tinty laying back her veil and waving, as the cab went down the drive towards the lodge gates.

"Margaret relented towards you at the end, almost as if she felt she was going to die," Tom observed to Marion as they stood waving at the top of the steps. Then, as it was opening time, he said good-bye himself and followed the cab down the drive on foot.

When Marion and Cassandra went indoors, only a lop-sided hen was left to enliven the façade, for Nanny and Mrs Adams had withdrawn their heads. The hen pecked between the cracks of the terrace paving stones and wandered into the hall. But as the dark shadows of indoors fell coldly across it like a knife, it turned and tottered back into the sunshine.

The first Virago Modern Classic was published in London in 1978, launching a list dedicated to the celebration of women writers and to the rediscovery and reprinting of their works. While the series is called "Modern Classics" it is not true that these works of fiction are universally and equally considered "great," although that is often the case. Published with new critical and biographical introductions, books appear in the series for different reasons: sometimes for their importance in literary history; sometimes because they illuminate particular aspects of women's lives, both personal and public. They may be classics of comedy or storytelling; their interest can be historical, feminist, political, or literary. In any case, in their variety and richness they promise to confuse forever the question of what women's fiction is about, while at the same time affirming a true female tradition in literature.

Initially, the Virago Modern Classics concentrated on English novels and short stories published in the early decades of the century. As the series has grown, it has broadened to include works of fiction from different centuries and from different countries, cultures, and literary traditions; there are books written by black women, by Catholic and Jewish women, by women of almost every English-speaking country, and there are several relevant novels by men.

Nearly 200 Virago Modern Classics will have been published in England by the end of 1985. During that same year, Penguin Books began to publish Virago Modern Classics in the United States, with the expectation of having some 40 titles from the series available by the end of 1986. Some of the earlier books in the series were published in the United States by The Dial Press.